If God Went to B-School

... Would love follow him there?

If God Went to B-School

... Would love follow him there?

Anand & Mani Ganesh

Srishti
PUBLISHERS & DISTRIBUTORS

SRISHTI PUBLISHERS & DISTRIBUTORS
N-16, C. R. Park
New Delhi 110 019
srishtipublishers@gmail.com

First published by Srishti Publishers & Distributors in 2010

3rd impression, 2012

This is entirely a work of fiction. All characters and events are totally imaginary.

Typeset in AGaramond 11pt. by Suresh Kumar Sharma at Srishti

Printed and bound in India

BOP. Forever.

Dedicated to our families,
our friends
and
our enemies

Acknowledgments

Grateful acknowledgments to the following (in no particular order):

To our blood relatives- Isha, Mom 1, Mom 2, Dad 1 & Dad 2 for reading the various drafts and versions and supporting this insanity

To Team BOP- Dharam, Rajat, Lisa, Shilpi & Varsha and all the other wonderfully weird people at FMS

To KV & Avtar for always being there

To the Kansal Group- Piyush, Sartaj, Kakkar, Kaushik, Sharma & Chowdhary

To the Kelas- Anshul, Ankit, Amit, Gagan, Bengali & Sikka

To Ms. Madhu Singh & Ms. Benedict for sparking this insanity years ago

To all our teachers

To God

Prologue

As I stepped out the gate, I looked back at the red brick building I was seeing perhaps for the last time. I wondered what life would have been had I not come here- had I not met the people I met, had I not seen humanity- naked & primordial and been simultaneously enchanted by its beauty & repulsed by its unsightliness; had I not lost so much to find myself.

My name is Hari Parmeshwar. This is my story. And if you have ever thought of or heard of or done an MBA, this is your story too.

City of Many Joys I

"Turn her over! TURN HER OVER!"

"Do… her… like… this," muttered a betel chewing one helpfully, pausing for suckling the betel of its juice and waving his arms wildly to explain the ideal process.

"You know, my sister-in-law who lives in Haldia has this way of doing it… ", pondered another one aloud smacking his lips lustily, "And she does it with tremendous gusto… not at all like you old chap."

I love Kolkata. It is the only city in the entire world where three people will set their own jobs aside and passionately advise a fellow being on the right way of doing things; in this case, frying a fish.

As I sat in my usual chair and enjoyed my usual fried fish and as the three Wise Men moved on to advising & supervising poor old Sujoy who was now preparing a *Mishthee Singhara*, I realized that I was addicted to the city. Addicted to the ubiquitous milling crowds, to the undying smell of putrid humid in the air, to the ridiculous ancientness of every standing edifice, to the almost scary array of talent that her people possessed, to the fact that nobody- no matter how dire the emergency- was ever in a hurry to get anywhere.

I looked out the half- open stained glass window and watched the organism called Kolkata breathe. Bipin- the colony gang boss harassing a street vendor. A dog, paralyzed by the heat, making weak attempts to shoo away flies with its tail. A bunch of school kids playing *gully* cricket. I smiled and whispered, "*I love you*" to the Kolkata beyond my window. And Kolkata- my mistress- ushered warm *loo* through the window- blowing me a kiss, hissing "*I love you too*" in my ear.

Our love story began four years ago with my flight landing at Dum Dum Airport. Kolkata looked at me through thick glasses. Kolkata smelled of sweat and heat and not of the fragrances women like to wear that nearly always succeed in activating my sinuses. Kolkata was hardly pretty, and even to the benevolent beholder- hardly beautiful; but to me, Kolkata was lovely.

Throughout my two months long on the job training at ABC Infotech in Bangalore, I didn't see much of her. She was a mystery to me- women always have been; but there was something divine to her mystery; something to her hair that I wished to drown in; something to her smell- her unflinching smell of Woman- that I wished to drink in. She spoke very little but whenever she did it was as if the very heavens wished to sing. Even though she did, my shyness and awkwardness with women ensured that she did not have a name. She was named yet nameless in Bangalore; in Kolkata nameless still, I named her Kolkata.

As weeks turned into months, I could still not muster the courage to ask Kolkata her name, to tell her she looked lovely or to tell her that her voice was music. She worked in a different department from mine at ABC and I hardly saw her twice or thrice a week (that too at a distance) but I- sad & doomed romantic- treasured those sightings of her. Perhaps the reader would find this hard to believe, but despite my mad love for her- I never once even tried to find out her name. It was as if once I found out what her name was, her mystery would end; and once she had rejected me- the unworthy lover- the magic would end. And I desperately wanted for the magic of Kolkata to never ever end.

Years passed and I fell deeper in love with her- both the city and the woman. Eventually, I came to know that her real name was Meenakshi and that she had a boyfriend, who worked in the same department as her. Heartbroken, I tried to reduce my sightings of her, to turn my thoughts on to what my mother called in her regular telephone calls "Making my Life". So, I got on to making my life. I asked my boss to put me on a project that would suck my lifeblood for no extra pay- something a lot of people do to beautify their CVs; only I did it to forget her, to move on. But nothing- not the extra hours at work, not the time I spent with my mistress- Kolkata- the city, nothing could make me forget her.

And then my mistress showed me the way. On my way to work one day I saw a huge crowd of what seemed like office goers, blocking traffic, gathered around what I presumed was some kind of miracle. I fought my way to the centre of the crowd and burst out laughing from what I saw. Two bulls were battling each other ferociously and the organism called Kolkata watched with no shred of fear or regard for being late for office. And thus she whispered in my ear- that there was nothing more important- not even the possibility of losing your life to trampling bulls, than doing what your heart wants.

So I went home that evening and started writing her a letter. Helped by Bipin's suspicious looking, smelling and tasting version of Vodka, I poured my heart out to her. I wrote of her hair, her beautiful smell, her voice made of music. And I wrote of Kolkata- the city and how I had fallen madly in love with both of them, the moment I saw them. And I wrote of how nothing- not even the bulls trampling me to death or her rejecting my proposal would ever make me love her any less.

"Hari-da, aur kuchh khaabe?"

I shook my head and paid Sujoy the twenty rupees I owed him for nourishing me with his heavily supervised version of Fish Fry. Sujoy gave me the special smile he reserved for old timers (which also happened to include the cooking supervisors) and said, "I hear FMS posted its written test results online yesterday. My cousin's son had no luck. Did you get through?" I shrugged. I didn't know. I didn't want to know. There seemed nothing more important than knowing that I had my first date with Meenakshi come Sunday.

The Interview

"*So, why do you want to become God?"*

He paused a little before answering, as if to give it some thought.

"Because it can't be without God."

"It?"

No pause this time.

"It... Life, Death- the whole bloody business."

"HARI PARMESHWAR!"

I found myself on a termite infested stool, doodling on a sheet of paper, with ten pairs of eyes staring at me. A searing pain rose through my upper arm where Mr. Anchor Shaped Goatee (I realized I had nicknamed him before embarking on the daydream) was elbowing me continuously, in harmonic motion. "Oye, isn't your name Hari?"

"HARI! HARI PARMESHWAR! Has he left?"

I closed my eyes and opened them again and as my grey cells

flickered to life, remembered that my name, as Mr. A. S. Goatee so eloquently put it, was indeed Hari Parmeshwar. I got up, blinked, stretched, yawned, straightened my tie, located the file housing my CV[1] (& some other documents), yawned again and drank a deep breath of the real world. I then found my way to the scrawny male uttering my name with genuine passion. "ARE YOU HARI PARMESHWAR?" he shouted as if I were at the other end of a long tunnel. I made a sound that approximated the affirmative and told him that he was blocking my way. I came across a knob that (compared to its fixture) seemed to have rusted prematurely, most likely from the sweat of several nervous pre- interview hands over the years. I pushed open the forbiddingly huge polished doors and stepped into a world of what seemed to be infinite bright.

Eyes blinking, heart racing, I took the four steps to the empty chair placed in the centre of the room. I wished the interview panel "Good Afternoon". The human being (christened Human One for hereafter) seated in the centre of the five member panel smiled and asked me to sit down. I placed my butt on the chair graced by hundred odd buttocks before me on the day; perhaps, even the same chair (considering the so called infrastructure constraints) on which the buttocks of the now rich & famous rested for 20 odd minutes of mind picking & verbal volleying. I tucked in my gut and smoothened my tie, hoping that it would hide the very recently acquired Sambhar stain on my shirt.

Human One: (*Without ceremony*) So, why do you want to become a Manager?

Me: (*Caught off guard & on Auto Pilot*) Because it can't be without a Manager.

---

[1] Curriculum Vitae

Human One: (*Puzzled*) *It*?

Me: (*Still on Auto Pilot*) Life, Death... (*Voice in Head to Me: WAKE UP ASSHOLE!*) Business... Um, I mean every... every functioning process in the world needs to be managed... And managers um... manage things.

Human Two: What kinds of things?

Me: (*After some thought*) All kinds of things.

At this point, Humans Two & Four started laughing openly. Humans Three & Five- women, gave the kind of dignified smile only women can manage. Human One's facial expression was inscrutable.

Human One: (*Sighing and looking at a piece of paper before him*) So what kind of "things" did you do in your four years at ABC InfoTech?

Me: Um...

I had done nothing worthwhile at ABC InfoTech... My career started on the bench where I did next to nothing- getting paid for just showing up and marking my attendance or writing oddball reports that nobody would read. Then, work hit me with full force. I was taken off the bench and ensnared by the banking services division to serve the remainder of my sentence, writing mindless code.

Me: I started off as a consultant, reviewing departments and their performance for ABC. (*In truth, I had written one very shitty report on the payroll division.*) Then I moved on to the BFSI (*Banking & Financial Services*) division of the business, where I worked on designing applications...

I will not bore the reader with the details of my career at ABC, not because of an inherent lack of sadism in my core but because the reader will have most likely lived or have had friends who have lived the IT[2]

[2]Information Technology

life- nay IT existence.

Human One: (*Looking at his watch*) Mr. Parmeshwar, to me, you look something of a rich man- maybe... a billionaire. So you topic for the extempore is... "Billionaire". You may start speaking.

Human Four gave a dilapidated looking stopwatch a theatrical bang and gestured for me to start. I began racking my brains for anything remotely related to billionaire but came up with nothing but a very inexplicable & disturbing image of a fat cow with a monkey's head. Unable to shake the hitherto unseen image from my head, I sputtered and managed to utter a few unintelligible noises, in what must have sounded like ParselTongue[3]*. At this point, Human One (clearly the Ringmaster of the circus) ordered me to "START NOW!"*

This sudden & incredibly loud utterance acted almost like a gunshot. Threatened and intimidated, my grey matter finally got into the act and my adrenaline stores relented, pumping the much needed drug through my veins. Consequently, I managed to utter a minute's worth of all the crap I could muster, on the subject of billionaire.

A few questions on all things IT followed. I realized that Human Three was conversant in every kind of plantation on Planet IT and challenged my diminished intellect to an extent. However, thankfully still a little high on adrenaline, I managed to muster a response for every query thrown at me.

Human Four: (*Speaking for the first time*) So son, why FMS? Why not the IIMs? Or XL?

Me: Because FMS is the only call I have.

Human Four: (*Smiling kindly)* Well, that makes matters incredibly simple, doesn't it?

---

[3] Snake Language

As I stepped out of the Room of Infinite Bright- the room I would later learn was called Sem Hall (Seminar Hall), I felt more alive and awake than I had ever in my life. Answers to questions I could not answer popped up in my head, names of billionaires I didn't utter in the extempore flashed before my eyes and better sounding ripostes-dripping with easy wit and political correctness, jingled in my ears. Freeing myself from the milling crowd begging me for a ball-by-ball of the interview, I descended down the stairs into a pall of gloom & Delhi's mad roads. I was sure that I had screwed up my only worthwhile B- School call in 5 years of giving CAT, XAT, MAT, SAT, FAT…

Even to this date and perhaps till the day I die, I will always recall with striking clarity two things about the interview.

One- the perennially pained weary expression on Human One's face.

And Two- that in my trance, I had doodled six very odd sentences on the CV I was carrying and as if to needlessly mock the uncanny seriousness of those weird sounding sentences, given my photo (on the CV) an Anchor Shaped Goatee.

15 Days of Hell

Sweat drenched his shirt and dripped off his nose, as he turned the knob and used his shoulder to force the door open. He did not bother to knock; though he was late, he knew he was expected. An old drone rose off from the recesses of the hall, "Ah… So, you have arrived."

I looked up from my notepad. An old drone rose off an old man on the stage "Let me tell you all that you have arrived! Faculty of Management Studies is the most…" I got back to my notepad.

Even though the man with the drone of a voice was clearly dying, he exuded an aura- which, though considerably weaker than before, made the already sweating man sweat even more. "Why is it not working?" the newcomer asked.

One of Matar's snores backfired noisily and he woke up to his own ruckus. "*Ghissu*, you taking notes already?" he mumbled and promptly went back to sleep, without waiting for my response. I'd met Matar or Manpreet Singh Tara, in my quest for rented accommodation near FMS campus. Due to its unique infrastructural constraints, FMS hostels could accommodate only about 40 to 50% of the batch. The rest of the batch would end up living in PGs[1] , flats or private hostels in Kamla Nagar, Vijay Nagar, Mukherjee Nagar or any of the ten or so Nagars abounding the North Campus area. Brought together in our quest for a residence by Pahalwan Properties, Matar and I ended up sharing a place about a kilometer away from campus.

As I resurfaced from my thoughts, I realized that the old drone had paused a while back. Exploiting the lull in his speech, a tsunami of applause rose from the back of the hall- where the second years sat. Several first years joined in- applauding lustily with whistling and hooting to boot. The speaker smiled and said something which got lost in the din. Finally realizing that he was being applauded off, he then uttered a "Thank You" and got off the stage, to much louder applause. A handsome young guy in a suit, with a somewhat pained expression on his face, then got on and asked the first years to introduce themselves to the Faculty.

Thus, the speeches of the old and distinguished were followed by the introductions of the new and the (largely) indistinguishable- the students. Turned out that our batch of hundred odd had a doctor, an ex army man, a Ranji playing cricketer, a football player from Bengal, an heir to the throne of some former Rajputana stronghold, two or three singers/ musicians, the predictable monstrous percentage of engineers (a handful from IITs, a few from NITs[2] & about 30 or so from DCE[3] / NSIT[4] - leading to scattered allegations that there was a

[1]Paying Guest accommodation

[2]National Institutes of Technology

[3]Delhi College of Engineering

[4]Netaji Subhash Institute of Technology

DCE quota at FMS) and a relatively decent quantity- about thirty- of females- that most sought after specie of any professional academic course.

I & Matar got talking to a few people over lunch- a wedding party style buffet. Everyone wondered what was to happen next. Whispers and rumors floated around- most of them involving varying degrees of mental and physical torture. Having gotten our plates and depressed ourselves with the thought of impending suffering, Matar & I sat in a corner - the only conversation passing between us being the sound of undignified ungentlemanly rapid munching of food.

The handsome young guy in the suit reappeared. "Juniors! You are to proceed from here to campus- Hall A. Be there by 2:00 pm sharp!"

I looked at my watch. It was 1:51 pm. Matar & I rushed outside and towards the aforementioned Hall A.

Hall A was huge & homely though slightly dilapidated. There were a few roof tiles that seemed to be in immediate danger of succumbing to gravity. Some of the chairs had had their cushions relished by pest infestations. The ACs ran rather reluctantly.

"...Just to remind you- this is not ragging. It's just an informal introduction. Anybody having a problem with this can walk out of the classroom now", the senior with a clipboard in her hands announced. Nobody moved.

"Well, seeing as that is settled...", she spoke again, this time consulting her clipboard, "Will the three Sardars please step forward?"

As the Sardars (which included Matar) performed synchronized bhangra to "Singh is King", I wondered what I would have to do to *informally introduce* myself. Sing? Serenade some girl? Pole Dance? Sell my half used pen to some senior? Or tell dirty jokes?

"Roll no. 30!" Woman with clipboard shouted.

I got up and walked to the front of the room. "First off, the three compulsory questions..." continued Clipboard Woman.

"Um... I don't smoke. I drink sometimes. And... um... I am not single."

The handsome suited male of the morning reappeared and made a gesture to Clipboard Woman that said "Enough". Clipboard Woman looked at her gold plated wristwatch and announced, "Okay it's six p.m. now. You are all to proceed to the Notice Board where details & groups for the next event of the day are posted. Form your groups and report to Sem Hall by 6:10. Come on... MOVE!"

A mad scramble for the notice board ensued, which contrary to Clipboard Lady's claims betrayed no details of the next event, except its name (MarCase) though it did divide hundred odd- very recently informally introduced beings- into groups. I discovered that I was in Group no. 8 which had 9 other humans besides me, none of whom I recognized by name. So I stood in a corner, shouting "Group 8!" at intermittent intervals. I saw Matar doing the same thing ("Group 2!") nearby.

My group finally formed five minutes later. Introductions were flung around and names exchanged & forgotten.

"PROCEED TO SEM HALL!" a fat senior bellowed. So we proceeded to Sem Hall.

The Sem Hall (or Seminar Hall) - the same room in which my interview had been held- was a cuboidal room with 3 giant perpendicular teakwood tables in the middle. At the head of the room, was a huge white screen, which was to liaise with a projector mounted on the roof. At the other end were two doors, one perennially locked; the other one being the heavily monitored solitary escape route from the room. It was about one tenth the size of the Convention Centre Hall- where the welcomings & speeches- the shenanigans of the day's morning had been held. And yet, inexplicably, it comfortably consumed and housed all hundred juniors leaving ample space for moving about. I felt as if I was in Arthur Weasley's magical tent.

5 seniors stood facing us at the head of the hall. "Welcome to FMS. And welcome to the Sem Hall," spoke the fattest male amongst them. "Hope you are having a great first day! We are MarkSoc- the marketing society at FMS and we have an event lined up for you. I hope everybody is sitting with their groups?" The Fat One paused to allow for some scrambling and jostling to take place. "Okay… we'll be distributing copies of a case. It's a one page case- not much. Basically, all groups have to go through the case and prepare a presentation on what the marketing mix should be like for the product. This is just to check whether you have been reading up on the marketing capsules we have been emailing you pre- session. You will have precisely 30 minutes to prepare your presentations and 10 minutes max to present. Any questions?"

Almost nobody in our group had gone through the marketing docs emailed by MarkSoc. There were two girls in the group who had gone through them but claimed not to have understood or remember much. So, we ended up making a generic ppt, which mostly repeated the case content itself. The final slide on marketing strategy (the question eventually posed in the case) carried such bullet points as:

- Make better product
- Sell more product
- Buy a company

- Leverage your strengths (*Point added at the behest of a group member who had read some Consulting Club document*)
- Learn from mistakes

Needless to say, ours was the worst ppt of the evening. The Fat One was close to tears while he shouted at us. "HAVE YOU GUYS NOT READ ANYTHING? 4Ps? STP? FRAMEWORKS? God… How are we going to place you guys?"

Later in the evening, the handsome young guy, now minus his suit, was addressing us in a calm tone, which betrayed disappointment. "Hi! I am Anand Muthu Swami, the General Secretary. You can call me Anand. I have been told by MarkSoc about your dismal performance in their case study event. Except one group, all the other presentations were shit." He paused for effect. "We have decided to give you all an opportunity to rectify your mistakes. MarkSoc is setting you another case study for the night. It will be emailed to your ids in half an hour. As you move outside, you'll find new groups posted on the notice board. Locate your team members. Sit together and discus the case. It's 9:15 now. The campus closes at 9:30. As your mentors might have told you, CCD and Barista are open till 11:30 pm. So you can gather there. Or gather at the residence at one of your team members. Or coordinate on phone. I don't care how you guys do it. I want the case solution mailed to my id by 5:59:59 am. Late and/ or shitty entries will be suitably penalized."

20 minutes later, I stood on the pavement outside the campus shouting "Group 3!" at intermittent intervals.

The guy with the incredibly anachronistic name recovered first. "What the fuck is this?"

Prabhjot raised a finger to his lips theatrically and shushed him. "Shhh... Let us finish it too."

Seven of us sat in a huddle around three laptops at the Café Coffee Day near the campus, trying to make sense of MarkSoc's latest case. It was an eighteen page treatise on P&G's merger with Gillette a few years ago. One of our group of eight had just disappeared and was incommunicado.

I had given up trying to understand the thing and was just looking dreamy eyed at the laptop screen, thinking of Meenakshi. I thought of the conversation we had had twenty minutes ago. I caressed my Nokia wishing it were her hand, wishing that she was not a million miles away in Kolkata. Her whispered "*Byeee*" still lingered in my ears.

I heard a loud guttural noise and looked up to find Prabhjot, having finally finished the bizarre piece of management literature, take a sip of his hitherto untouched iced tea. He stopped mid-sip, pointed his finger at the laptop screen and articulated, "What the fuck *is* this?"

I looked at my watch. It was 8:50. We were getting late for the 9:00 AM class.

"FMS? *Ye kya hai*?" wondered the rickshawallah, scratching his chin.

"Faculty of Management Studies... *MBA college hai bhaiyya*" Matar replied.

"MBA? *Ye kya hai?*" More chin scratching ensued. Matar laughed.

"Dude forget it… let's just walk" I offered.

"No, wait… I have an idea", began Matar. "*Bhaiyya, yeh Kirori Mal to jante ho na? Uske opposite hai.*"

"Dus Rupay", the rickshawallah offered. *"FMS… FMS… Koi naya college hoga…"*

Both of us fell asleep as soon as the rickshaw started its journey. We had slept for barely three hours the previous night having spent time with our respective groups in solving the case. In addition, we had received email communiqués at about 2 AM in the night about a one page write up- on marketing frameworks, to be submitted individually ("*No Cut- Copy- Paste Allowed!"*) to MarkSoc by 9 AM.

Prabhjot had insisted we shift base to his PG once CCD kicked us out at 11:30, which most of us did. After Prabhjot had emailed our shady riposte to the case, I left his PG for mine at about 4 am. I had come home to find Matar sleeping with his head on his laptop's keyboard.

The rickshawallah woke us up at FMS gates. "*Yehi hai kya?*"

Matar nodded groggily. I didn't really care.

I slept through the entire first class. Matar woke me up for the roll call.

As the Prof left, a buzz spread across the room. I heard someone shouting out my name. "HARI! Come here!" I looked around to find Jaidev, one of my group- mates from last night shouting my name. "Hari! You are in my Group." "Yeah dude, we mailed the case solution yesterday… don't you remember?" I replied. "No man, this new FinSoc event has just been floated and emailed to us. You are in my group again. Group 11."

"NOBODY BUNKS ANY CLASSES!" Anand was shouting at us.

I did not know what day it was. I did not know if it was day or night. Time had ceased to exist; ceased to matter.

"And nobody bloody misses any MSA events! This hectic schedule is designed to induct you into a tough life. If you do have to miss either, you mail me the reason and I will choose whether to grant you an exemption or not. Otherwise, you'll have to pay up a thousand bucks for every session you miss and explain yourselves to the PlaceCom."

The PlaceCom is the most revered and feared body on any B-School campus. Their proximity to the primary goal of an MBA education, i.e. placement, makes them the one body no one wishes to have even the slightest disagreement with.

"Bear in mind, this schedule, the events & the GLs being conducted are to prepare you for your summer placements. Your summer interviews are barely three months away. Take everything very seriously! If you do not, I assure you- YOUR SUMMERS WILL BE HAMPERED!"

"Let my fucking summers be fucking hampered!"

We were probably ten days into the induction fortnight. I had not bathed more than twice in the last ten days. (By my estimates, Matar had not bathed at all.) This one day I had not had the time (or the energy) to answer nature's calls at all. Classes & MSA[5] events persisted from 9AM to beyond 9:30 PM, with breaks affording a maximum of twenty minutes in between.

One of the sadistic old Profs had set us a 200 page case with

[5]Management Science Association-the nodal student body at FMS

recommended additional readings. Another one had set us a 50 question assignment. Anand & his MSA gang were killing us with an average of three submission deadlines in a day. To cap it, if you had three MSA submissions in a day, you were in three different groups making any kind of coordination and/ or team meetings virtually impossible.

To make my life worse, my conversations with Meenakshi had gotten shorter & brusquer as the week progressed. She had kept on badgering me to describe in the minutest possible detail every friend I had made on campus. She had outright rejected my claim that I had made no female friends on campus and constantly bemoaned that it was only a matter of time before I found someone better than her. Most of my conversations with her were spent in building the notion that FMS had really ugly females and my only long term intention of engagement with any of these ugly females was to get a *Rakhi* tied on my wrist. Instead of being refreshed by her musical voice- as I had been on my first day at FMS, the conversations were beginning to extract a toll on me- my dark circles had gotten distinctly darker; I had found a grey hair in my sideburns.

The only happy highlight of the past ten days had been the Red Bull babes- one of the details I had conveniently omitted in my descriptions of the environment to Meenakshi. The Red Bull babes had entered the Sem Hall and our life- during a ConClub[6] GL, to distribute free Red Bull cans amongst us. They had worn light blue denim mini skirts and tight red tops (one size too short) and were (for a sleep deprived male dominated batch- also deprived of several other *releases*) the most beautiful creatures God ever created. Seventy odd pairs of masculine gazes followed their every hypnotic move,

[6]Consulting Club

the subtle movements their slight bodies afforded, the way their luscious lips parted when they said, "Enjoy!" or "Thank You". The GL[7] was suspended for twenty odd minutes while the Red Bull Babes & associated tomfooleries persisted. When they left the hall finally, seventy pairs of male eyes looked longingly at the door.

"Dude, are you even fucking listening? I said let my fucking..." Matar hollered.

"Yeah Matar, I'm listening" I replied. This was one of our rare lucky nights. For the first time, Matar and I were in the same two member group for the assignment that had to be emailed by 5:59:59 AM.

"Let's fucking fuck this fucking assignment. We'll fucking pay the fucking thousand bucks. Let's just fucking go to fucking sleep."

I did a quick cost benefit analysis in my head, which told me that I would be willing to pay a million bucks for six hours of continuous sleep. So we fucking fucked the fucking assignment and slept.

"DO YOU THINK WE ARE JOKERS?" Madhavan bellowed.

I sat facing the firing squad in my mandatory PlaceCom interaction of Hell's Fortnight. Madhavan was the Placement Secretary. And Madhavan was bellowing at me. When Madhavan bellowed at you, you wished you were a tortoise and you could retreat into your shell & hide. Two of his gang members sat facing me, giving me menacing looks- daring me to call them "Jokers".

"You think it's okay to miss assignment deadlines?" The PlaceComie called Girija asked. A quiet anger lingered in her voice.

"No ma'm, it was only this one time. Actually..."

[7]Gyaan Lecture

Azhar cut me short. "And what is this atrocity of a CV you have submitted?"

"You see I just had thirty minutes to submit a one page CV. As I did not get time to edit it, I merely submitted the first page of my three page CV" I offered.

"SHOULD WE EVEN ACCEPT THAT AS AN EXCUSE?!" The bellowing started again.

Eventually, I gave in. I accepted that I was a joker; that my CV was a sham; that my reason was an excuse. There was nothing left to say anymore. My communal rape was over. My rapists were satiated. They let me go.

I met Mowgli- my mentor in the senior batch on my way to the Sem Hall from my interrogation room. "PlaceCom Interaction?" he asked. I nodded in reply.

Mowgli laughed. "You look terrible. Have some water. Wash your face. It's really not as bad as they must have told you."

"But they told me I didn't belong here" I said.

Mowgli grew pensive. "Well, they say that to a lot of people- don't worry. In fact, it is the truth. Not many of us do belong here. Look at your batch- cricketers, trained dancers, musicians- how many of you do belong here? We all come here leaving behind the things we love… things which might pay us one tenth of what we'll get after an MBA but doing which we were a thousand times happier."

I looked at Mowgli's sad face and wondered what he had left behind for this. "So, sources tell me you have a girlfriend stashed away somewhere…" Mowgli began.

"Yup, I do."

Mowgli smiled. "Just something to wreck your day further. 75%

of pre- FMS affairs end in breakups during first year. The rest end in second year."

I laughed at the impossible odds. "So basically I have no hope?" I wondered.

Mowgli laughed again. "Nope... none."

By the fifteenth day, everyone smelled except this one female called Shraddha who somehow found time to bathe and put on (among other things) an atrocious purple eye shadow every day. By the fifteenth day, the Profs had stopped kicking out people who slept in class. By the fifteenth day, I had learnt how to Cut- Copy- Paste clever and how to hide behind as one group member gave the presentation I knew nothing about. By the fifteenth day, the sun had set 15 times without me having seen it. By the fifteenth day, Meenakshi was farther away from me, than she had been when Hell started.

As the last event of the last day of Hell's Fortnight ended, FMS lawns erupted into impromptu celebrations. As speakers blared with loud Bollywood music and as Matar & I danced & hugged & laughed & screamed, I hung on to my one happiness in my heart made of sad- that I had one full night of sleep ahead of me.

[illegible]

[illegible]

[illegible] the [illegible]

[illegible] Delhi [illegible] [illegible]

[illegible] in my second group of Hells [illegible] was [illegible] he had had an incredibly anachronistic [illegible]

"[illegible] Lal Madho", he extended his [illegible] digits towards my [illegible]

[illegible]

[illegible] The big [illegible] [illegible] Lal paused [illegible]

<3

I sat with my head in my hands, looking into the distance, praying for my sinus initiated headache to recede.

"Dude, that's going to take some work..."

I looked up to find a tall paper- thin guy who had happened to be in my second group of Hell's Fortnight. All I remembered was that he had had an incredibly anachronistic name.

"Banwarilal Madho", he extended his bony digits towards my bonny ones for a handshake. "Or BanMad, as the chicks call me."

I smiled and shook BanMad's hand. "Me Hari Parmeshwar... What's going to take some work?"

"You were looking at her weren't you, you lovesick puppy? Neelima or as I prefer to call her- T-B-B ... The Big Bong." BanMad paused for that to sink in. "She's a 9.75 on the BanMad scale of female hotness." He eyed her top to bottom, in what seemed an experienced, practiced, even professional gaze. "She's got a boyfriend of course... but her pink slippers tell me she's looking for some well (*cough cough*) male companionship."

I looked at BanMad with the most puzzled expression my facial muscles could muster.

"You clearly have lots to learn. Well, watch and learn my friend!" And just as suddenly as he had reappeared in my life, BanMad- the guy with the incredibly anachronistic name, got up and disappeared into the crowd that was beginning to form again in the Sem Hall.

I met him again at Sem Hall doors after the GL ended. "Damn GL had to start just when I had started working on her. But we are off to a flyer my dear friend," BanMad assured me confidently, beaming. "She said I was cute… like Scooby Doo."

"His name is Manpreet Singh Tara. He is my roommate. I told you about him before, remember?"

Matar yelled raunchily "Haaaai Meenooooo".

I tried unsuccessfully to prevent Matar's response from being captured by my damn Nokia.

"No no, Sweets… that was some vegetable seller… they have really loud voices," I offered Meenoooo in damage control. "And the other one is Banwari. I told you about him too, remember? He is the engineer from DCE… who worked in Maruti for two years. Yes… yes."

BanMad/ Scooby laughed. "HP! Tell her I am twice as handsome as you!"

This time I *was* successful in preventing transmission of Scooby's remark.

"No Sweets… no girls at all. I swear… Just a simple dinner for the three of us. I am not lying... I promise you na... Yes yes, I'll call you after... No sweets, nobody is laughing." I offered the guffawing Matar and Scooby my most intense pleading look.

"Bye Sweets. Miss you." I hung up, sighing.

Matar still shaking with laughter, walked up to me, held me by my shoulders and in an approximation of what he thought was Meenakshi's voice asked demurely, "Love you too *Sweets*... Can we go to dinner now?"

The dinner actually did involve girls. It was supposed to be a gastric celebration of the apparent End of Hell. And Scooby of course thought that no celebration could be complete if the opposite gender wasn't involved. So five apparently single females, averaging 8 on the "BanMad Scale of Female Hotness" were invited. In Scooby's words (to his target group of the five 8's on the BM Scale) - "It is going to be legendary."

Eventually, it was anything but that. Two females turned up (an 8.5 & a 9 on the Scale) and to Scooby's great disappointment brought male friends along. One of them actually turned up with her boyfriend- whom she funnily kept referring to as her "friend". The other guys were Prabhjot & Mithun, who we later found out had overheard Scooby inviting one of the females and had simply tagged along with Ruchi (the 9).

After a lot of brain cells were consumed/ immolated in figuring out a place where eight people could sit and dine, we ended up in Udupi- a South Indian restaurant in the North Campus area. Further grey cells were killed in deciding what should be had for dinner (even though South Indian restaurants offer an obvious limited choice). By the time dinner arrived the group had broken into sub groups- Aastha & her "friend"; Mithun, Prabhjot & Ruchi (Mithun and

Prabhjot had sat on either side of Ruchi thwarting Scooby's best laid plans) and finally, me, Matar and a rather disgruntled looking Scooby.

Delhi too, looked disgruntled in August. It was hot & humid and when it rained, August flooded the streets and spawned a million insects. You just couldn't fight August and her temper... the heat found you in the shade, made the bath water hot & ineffective and rendered our PG's desert cooler- a mere circulator of air.

As hot & stormy as the weather was the love scene at FMS. A few break ups (pre- FMS relationships) were reported. Two couples moved in together (one couple- make up queen Shraddha and a guy named Rajansh- during induction itself). Several one night stands were claimed (mostly by males) and rubbished as rumors; a few were established to a degree of belief and discussed at length by almost everybody in almost every break. And a large majority of the male population became frustrated one sided lovers (FOSLA's).

Prominent among the FOSLA's was a chap called Vineet who had fallen quite madly in love with Ruchi and was leaving no stone unturned in attempting to woo her. Now Vineet was a simpleton- an engineer with work ex- the son of a Brahmin temple priest from a village in UP while Ruchi was a "city babe"- a fresher from across the road (Kirori Mal). Even to the most creative/ liberal mind who believes in the blindness of love or the absence of social critique in love, they were a rather unlikely couple.

And this was perhaps the reason that Vineet's love for the Kirori Mal damsel became one of the legendary stories on campus despite the persistence of innumerable such male one- sided afflictions. Entire email threads were devoted to "*99's love for 64*" (the unlikely couple's roll numbers) and when Vineet bid a record 8000 Rupees for a date with Ruchi in Silent Auction (a clever means for monetizing on-campus tomfooleries- to donate money to charity), it became one of the headlines in The Times of India ("*A date for 8000 at FMS*"). As it turned out, the date never really materialized.

In the midst of August's tempers, with Hell's Fortnight three weeks gone, life was still not that far from hell. GLs, random events & projects persisted. The only difference was that we were now free from MSA imposed groups (and free to form our own ones) and deadlines/ assignments averaged one every three days (as opposed to three every day during Hell). This brought a taste of freedom, which being considerably lesser than our halcyon days on our jobs or in our undergraduate courses, was revered and treasured with a vengeance.

So if we had thirty minutes (sometimes even a luxurious sounding hour) between sessions, we generally made the most of it, rushing to Anna's (FMS contracted canteen guy) or to the Delhi School of Economics Canteen where the food was much better. We- Matar and me (occasionally accompanied by Scooby and his women- Ruchi and/ or Aastha and their devout followers/ devotees- Mithun and Prabhjot)- were discovering new & cheap- with *cheap* being the watchword- eateries around campus. We discovered a Bhelpuri guy opposite St. Stephens, a Chhole Bhature guy near Arts Faculty and a momos guy in Kamla Nagar. The Chhole Bhature guy soon became our favorite (mine & Matar's at any rate) and his ten rupee plate of rustic Chhole Bhature became our staple food.

It was whilst we were eating Chhole Bhature one day, that Matar asked me, "HP, Meenakshi… why do you love her?"

Coming from someone else, I might have considered the question too personal- too weird, perhaps even taken offence. But this was

Matar.

I shrugged. "I do not know, man. But I guess she's the first woman who's made me feel this way." I paused to think. "Perhaps I am wrong. Perhaps I am simply in love with the idea of being in love."

Matar did not reply or ask me anything further. We just ate our ten rupee plates in silence.

It was me who broke the silence a few minutes later.

"*She is a thing of beauty*

but not a joy forever.

She is a moment's respite

in this city of blinding lights."

Matar smiled and nodded.

We were down to our last bites when Scooby materialized, holding out his mobile in front of him. "There's a session at 2:30. Move it comrades! Or we'll miss the best seats in the house."

The best seats in Sem Hall were behind the pillar on the left. You were completely invisible to the guy/ guys in the front as also- by a neat trick of physics- always in comparative shade even with all the lights on. The area had come to be referred as X- Ray corner (because you had to have X- Ray vision to see through the pillar- to see what was going on in the front) or alternately as ChillSoc Corner- ChillSoc being the term (coined by a creative Nepali called Dharmesh) for an unofficial society, devoted entirely to the task of chilling out.

"I hope it's not one of those fucking FinSoc[1] sessions... All those dudes care about is showing off before the batch babes" Matar said.

"And MarkSoc sessions? Aren't they almost always all gas?" I asked.

[1]Finance Society

"Naah, I like them... And they show us some real cool ads" Matar retorted chuckling.

"I would take a MarkSoc session any day" Scooby chipped in. "Have you noticed the twins on Shipra? I could stare at them for hours and hours without caring about what shit she's speaking." Scooby receded into his private dreamland for a while, where I imagine he was accompanied by Shipra's voluminous assets.

"Anyway, it's neither MarkSoc nor FinSoc or actually... it's both and more" Scooby said, returning from his reverie. "Gentlemen, we now have society presentations."

Half an hour later, in the Sem Hall, Anand started the proceedings. "The society presentations are a means for societies to tell you what they do. Then you guys can make an informed decision about which society you want to join. There are two kinds of posts in societies- selected and elected. I'll tell you guys later about the application procedure, selection, election, etc. First, listen to what the societies have to say. Any questions?" Anand looked around to find a solitary hand go up in the air.

It was Mithun who said "Yeah, Anand, I have a question."

"Go ahead."

Mithun got up, cleared his throat rather theatrically, straightened the collar on his shirt and began "Anand, are... are m... mem... members of the E- Cell- the entrepreneurship society- eligible for placements?"

"What! Of course they are! Why would they not be?"

"Because" Mithun began dreamily, "Enterpreneurs create jobs... n... not seek them." And then he looked around for adulation as if he had made the quote of his life. In the ChillSoc corner, Matar and I bent over laughing.

"Mithun, are you superdumb? This is the twentieth time you have asked me or a Soc a stupid obvious question. If you ever again ask a senseless question, I will kick your ass. Now sit the fuck down!"

Mithun sat down like a deflated bubble.

"Any more questions? No? Good… first up is MarkSoc." Scooby's posture changed suddenly to one of rapt attention.

"So 101 people and all they have is 51 posts?"

Matar smiled. "That's fucking plenty man. Not everybody's gonna apply. I overheard some of the 8 by 8 babes saying they were too tired of all the MSA bullshit to apply."

8 by 8, Kamla Nagar was the address of the most populated private hostel for FMS females. Everybody knew where 8 by 8 was, especially people who didn't live there.

"Yeah, but…"

"Look here, Hari my man- we'll apply- then whether we get through or not is up to Wahe Guru. So calm down."

"Matar, you don't get it… Six months… You are almost a fresher. I have waited four years for this. I don't want to screw anything up. I want to do this MBA right."

Matar sighed. "So, apply to all the fucking Socs. You are sure to get lucky with one."

I ended up applying to five societies/ clubs- ConClub, SysSoc[2], Media[3], MarkSoc[4] & FinSoc- after my (perhaps inevitable) eventual

[2]Systems Society

[3]Media Relations Cell

[4]Marketing Society

rejection in the preliminary rounds of junior PlaceCom formation. Matar proceeded to the final round of PlaceCom formation- the election- but lost out there. He thereafter, applied to just two societies- Media Relations & MarkSoc. Scooby applied to all the societies with hot babes in them.

The initial rounds of most Socs' selection procedures were some kind of group activities. I got rejected by FinSoc and SysSoc in the group stage itself. Especially funny was the FinSoc group activity, which was actually a GD on a weird financial term that I could barely pronounce let alone speak on. It ended up being a two way discussion between two Eco graduates from Stephens, who could both pronounce and speak on the topic.

For the next round of selection/ rejection, most societies then released forms with questions like "*Why should MarkSoc take you?*" and "*What new initiatives do you think ConClub should take up this year?*" Some forms required data to be dug up, like Media Relations- which asked for media contacts with their phone numbers. Torn between my desire to make a Soc- any Soc at all and the mental fatigue from filling up lengthy forms, digging up data and thinking up different answers to similar questions like "*What makes you unique?*", I finally ended up copy- pasting (with minor modifications) Matar's Media and MarkSoc answers. I wrote some of my school friends' phone numbers in media contacts and asked them to moonlight as bogus reporters if any calls reached them.

The next round was one- on- one interviews with the Socs. Media and MarkSoc had already rejected me on the basis of my shady application forms. All that was left was ConClub, which had been my first preference anyway.

I eventually did get through ConClub. Shikhar, one of the seniors who had taken my interview, later told me that it had been my desperation (to get into the Soc) that had made me stand out. Matar got Media Relations (he cleared MarkSoc too but Media had been his first preference). Scooby got Praxis (the HR Soc) - the society which had incidentally seen the least applications (eight applications for five posts) and what with three female Praxis seniors who figured quite high on the BM Scale, Scooby was quite confident of finding love.

City of Blinding Lights

Delhi is not a city of love or of joy. It is impossible to describe it as one whole being; it is rather a crude mix of several beings- a splinching together of the souls of all the small towns and other cities people come here from. And it is most unlike Kolkata which you can fall in love with.

Rather, Delhi is a city you make a truce with. You hate the extreme weather, you hate the traffic jams, you hate the average Delhiite on the road- who's always looking to make a quick buck (at your expense) and yet you make a truce because clearly, Delhi is the best that India can do. I found everyone looking to create their own island of truce in this city of hate.

August's tempers and storms made the City of Hate madder. Roads were ravaged, trees mutilated, streets flooded, power cables uprooted. The city, like almost every other in the country, ended up raped by a few centimeters of rainfall. And the people in their anger and madness turned their anger not at the rapists- the bureaucrats or the politicians but at each other. I witnessed pitched battles between car owners whose machines had, perhaps in a moment of perverse passion, been unfortunate enough to nudge each other. Residents of a nearby colony set a bus afire when they fell prey to a 48 hour long power cut.

The amazing thing about Delhi was that unlike Kolkata, nobody cared to stop and stare. People drove past sparring car owners and buses aflame (albeit a little slowly). There was perhaps too much adventure in every individual's life for the city to come together and have a collective adventure. In Kolkata, a bus on fire would have been the day's entertainment; in Delhi it was simply that- a bus on fire.

After a while, it got to you- the nonchalance, the culture of anger and hate. It sat itself in your head like a monster who pecked at your brain and ate and slept there, without paying rent.

"Hari, have you fucking checked you email lately?"

I had just received a rather disquieting message on my mobile and my energies were diverted. So, I just nodded and mumbled something unintelligible.

"RESERVE YOUR PARSELTONGUE FOR FUCKING SNAKES!" Matar took a deep breath and then resumed. "Why the fuck did we register, man?'

Agitated, I shot back "For what, bhenchod?"

"War Room."

It took me over a minute to exhume the memory labeled 'War Room'. War Room was a business competition that had been floated by Mahindra & Mahindra in our initial month on campus. Enamored by the company presentation, enticed by the huge monetary reward and childishly upbeat about our chances of creating a fantabulous business presentation, we had registered for the event on the spot and then, in the ensuing madness that the first month of first year meant, promptly forgotten about it. I recalled that along with Matar and me, our four member team for the event comprised of Scooby and an unknown entity, whom Scooby had brought to the table (necessitated by the rest of our "legendary Udupi dinner" group- Aastha, Ruchi, Prabhjot and Mithun forming their own separate team).

"Dude, society selections just ended. I haven't slept more than five hours in the last few days." Remembering a certain induction assignment, I said smiling, "Let's fucking fuck the fucking event and go to sleep."

Matar sighed. "Dude, we are the fuckees- not the fuckers this time. Placement Convener just emailed all War Room participants. Mail says that all first year teams have fucking defaulted on entry submissions. M&M is pissed. We have to submit our entries within the next 24 hours or Convener says we'll be barred from summer placements."

I looked at the message which like Delhi's monster sat in my mobile, pecking at my head without paying rent. "Damn man... Why did we register?"

The message did it. I was Hari Parmeshwar- perpetual romantic, disgruntled software engineer, of Kolkata's love. And I was Hari Parmeshwar- intermittent romantic, disgruntled MBA student, of Delhi's truce. The disjoint between the two worlds- the lack of fit- that had been simmering under the surface, boiled over and spilled. It made a soft pop- virtually unnoticeable.

It made everything- the general chaos, the lack of sleep, the miserable monotony of Guest Lectures, the shady ppt we made for

War Room prelims, the long one and a half hour classes, Anna's inconsistent food- irrelevant. I was the zombie of Delhi going through the motions of an MBA without thinking/ feeling- making ppts, listening to people go on & on about marketing or finance or summers and I was Meenakshi's love, lost in MBA's jungle.

Nothing registered- marketing or finance, boredom or interest, cold or heat, food or pain, Matar or Scooby. My mouth answered queries, forged replies; my eyes witnessed without observing; my ears heard without listening. I forgot how to feel- accumulated every emotion in a box for Delhi's monster to feed on.

The message did it. It said simply, "Coming to Delhi on 15th Aug. C ya. Meena." And as soon as it did, I was lost- I was neither of Delhi nor of Kolkata- but caught in between. The only sight I remembered was of the message on my mobile screen- the only sound I heard was of Delhi's monster in my head, feeding on my unregistered emotions, growing bigger and stronger.

I was submerged- neither sinking nor floating. I was under the surface- unable to breathe yet unable to drown.

By the time I woke up on the 15th- my first holiday at FMS, Matar had already left. He had pasted a Post- It on our room's solitary crack infested mirror which said "Left for aunt's place. C u!" I do not know how he knew. Maybe I had mentioned it; maybe he had read the message on my mobile.

I sat on the bed feeling sleepy yet beyond sleep. So I got up and walked to the balcony where I hadn't ever had time to stand and watch the drama of everyday Delhi life unfold under me. But it was 7 and it was a national holiday; Delhi & its drama were both, as yet, asleep.

The exhaustion I thought I had successfully evaded, returned with a vengeance. It swept me off my feet and onto my creaking bed. As Delhi began to wake up around me, I went back to sleep.

I dreamt as I slept. I dreamt that I was a fish- a fish in water more blue than I had ever seen. It was so blue that I could barely see, barely make out the surface above me. As I swam, I came across nothing but the blueness of the sea- there was no other sensation- nothing else existed or mattered. And then I began to drown, my gills melted, my fins became of leather. I was drowning, sinking, knowing that death was near- that fighting it was futile. I had just made peace with my destiny that something rescued me, something pulled me out of death's blue, into a morning so colorful and pleasant that I laughed.

My savior held me in a jar- from where I saw strange sights. I saw a bull and a car wrestle each other. I saw three wise men shouting out advice to the combatants. I saw Sujoy and the mole on his left cheek. I saw in the distance, myself- Hari the human- ordering a fish fry and Sujoy's subtle nod. And then, Sujoy's hand reaching for my jar. In a swooping motion, he thrust me into the frying pan where burning oil sat, smacking its lips lustily, waiting for its latest victim.

I felt pain beyond pain. Yet death would not come and salvage me. Sujoy's ladle fished for me in the oil and rescued me from its wrath momentarily; destined to be thrust again into oil's painful embrace. But for a moment, destiny conspired; Sujoy's practiced swoop failed; I flailed through the air- not into the frying pan but into the fire. I was a fish- ravaged by oil, next by fire. I was a proverb Meenakshi would read off her mobile's screen.

And then I was served to Kolkata's Hari, who sat at the window and treasured Kolkata's kisses. I was a fish out of water- ravaged and raged- Delhi's Hari. I stood in my bowl and screamed "HARI! IT'S

ME! HARI, DON'T! IT'S ME!"

But Hari was lost in Kolkata's kisses and love's labors. I shouted again, "Hari! Wake up! It's me" But Hari was lost, fast asleep, in his own world. He looked out the window as he plunged his fork straight for my heart.

"HARI! WAKE UP!"

I woke up. I rubbed my eyes trying to rid them of the bizarre dream they had just seen. She sat beside me, on the bed, wearing a worried expression on her face. "You OK?" There sat my music; my unflinching scent of Woman; my love. Meenakshi- my fish eyed love, looked at me and smiled. My senses dulled; my eyes blinded, my nose, my ears, my skin all seemed to wither away like petals off a dying rose. Her smile did it.

I gave in. I was Delhi's monster- August's Storm, stripped of all time, all sense of being, all reality- I was every emotion that I had not felt in the days since I got her message. I watched as the monster kissed Meenakshi fiercely; as he held her tight in his embrace.

She protested initially but then she gave in. The monster was relentless- he kissed her on her lips, he kissed her beautiful eyes, he bit her neck. And when she smiled, he kissed her smile.

The monster undid her shirt's buttons. I would not listen to her protests, I could not- I was beyond all sense. When she whispered "Please, Hari…" in my ear, I kissed her lips more, kissed her plea and her worrying eyes. I ran one hand through her hair and kissed her forehead and her nose and her neck and tightened my embrace as I kissed her.

She gave in. We lay in the creaking bed- Kolkata's lovers in the midst of Delhi's madness. I felt her breath mingle with mine as we made love. I kissed the pearl drops of sweat that formed on her forehead. The monster devoured her as I watched and I petted her where the monster hurt. And then for one moment, everything around us dissolved; the monster spent itself and I was Hari again, no longer sinking nor floating. I was rid of the madness of Delhi, the Storm of August- and I was the Hari I had been once. I smelt her hair, felt her breath on my cheek, I listened to her heart thump against its cage. I felt alive again.

She looked at me with a sad worried look in her eyes. I smiled, kissed her forehead and caressed her cheek. I looked right into her eyes and said, "I love you." Her sadness dissolved, her eyes became the clear light brown they were and she smiled.

The next morning, after my fish eyed lover had left, Delhi ceased to bother me. It was as if now that I knew who I was, I had made peace with the fact that I could never belong to Delhi's madness. I was Hari Parmeshwar; perpetual romantic. Of Kolkata. Lost in Delhi. I slept peacefully for the first time since I came to FMS.

The sun shone brighter and fiercer; the sky was redder than blue; crows cawed their throats hoarse and roads developed cracks and puddles for cars to injure themselves in. But I found beauty in Delhi' scars; music in Delhi's cacophonies. I saw, smelt and heard Meenakshi everywhere. Every sensation was an extension of her. Perpetual romanticism.

And it was in this frame of mind that I met Bastard.

[illegible]

[illegible] I looked [illegible] [illegible] [illegible]

[illegible]

in case I'll disappear.

She looked at me [illegible] and [illegible] look in her eyes. I [illegible] her hand [illegible] of her neck. I looked [illegible] [illegible] the [illegible] we were in one another.

The [illegible] [illegible] I [illegible] [illegible] [illegible] I could never [illegible] [illegible] I kept practicing for the [illegible] came [illegible]

[illegible] other hand [illegible] [illegible] [illegible] [illegible] and I heard [illegible] [illegible] Perpetual [illegible]

[illegible] in the [illegible] [illegible] that I [illegible]

[illegible]

Kinetic Kids

How or when he came be known as Bastard was debatable. Prima facie he was not of illegitimate origin; so the dictionary meaning did not apply. Matar believed one of the 8 by 8 chicks had christened him that after he had (allegedly) given her a rather colorful tongue lashing during Induction. Scooby, on the other hand, believed he had punched one of the seniors in the face, when he had tried to rag him and hence, had been christened by the seniors as such. And there were a few other versions of the story on campus. Anyhow, it caught on and the guy became (& responded to) Bastard.

The plastic table at Anna quivered slightly as Bastard- the hitherto unknown entity of our War Room team- twirled a pen rather violently between his fingers. A pensive look occupied Bastard's face as he sipped something out of a plastic cup, apparently digesting the piece of news that had shocked all of us, in small sips. Matar, who was not built for small sips or thoughtful introspection, was panting as he recuperated from shock and his initial reactionary stream of involuntary swearwords. Scooby had been taking out his anger on inanimate things; currently he was mutilating his Vada with a passion.

Matar's shock spilled over into speech, again. "How the fuck did we qualify?"

To our collective shock and awe, we figured among the fourteen teams that had been selected for the campus finals of War Room out of the 30 odd teams of four that had registered.

"Twenty minutes… We made that ppt in fucking twenty minutes. And what was our idea? Yes… A rural bike! What the fuck's a rural bike!"

"It is a bike for villages. And, calm down man." Bastard spoke for the first time, the pen still a-twirl on his digits.

"DON'T TELL ME TO FUCKING CALM DOWN! I will not calm down! You know what our selection means?"

Bastard nodded subtly.

"No you don't! It means we have to give our fucking twenty minute ode to shadiness to a senior management team from M&M. So, prepare yourselves for a grand royal public fucking!"

We wore suits and ties for what Matar had perhaps prophetically described as our *grand royal public fucking*. Most of our presentation had been plagiarized from a site called scribd.com and then given cosmetic surgery. We didn't have a cash inflow/ outflow plan- none of us understood finance that well. While teams around us were struggling to fit in extra information (into their on average thirty slide presentations), our mantra was to speak as slowly as possible to fill the fifteen minutes allotted- with our nine slide ppt. To cap it all, our team was called Kinetic Kids (name picked by Scooby), which (in Bastard's words) made us sound like a 70's Swedish porno flick.

Our presentation finished in seven minutes flat. Scooby (who opened) got nervous and ran through his slides very quickly. This gave the presentation an intangible underlying tempo that Matar and I both subconsciously adhered to, running through seven of our nine slides at record pace. Bastard, who was to close, tried to salvage us somewhat by going through his slides extremely slowly. I noticed he was an excellent speaker; he moved, gestured & used the space around him with an elegant professional ease and held people to rapt attention even though he was professing our shitty nonsense.

Our ppt ended to utter silence. I heard one clap emanate from the far corner of the Sem Hall; although in all probability it was somebody trying to decimate a mosquito. For two minutes, none of the judging panel (comprised of three executives from M&M) spoke. The oldest of the lot recovered first. "So you are going to make an Italian design bike for Indian villages and price it at 10000 bucks? (*Cough*)Um... How?"

We, of course, didn't know how. Matar, Scooby and I stood looking at each other, hoping for someone to come up with something. Bastard stood in the other corner, nonchalantly twirling a pen, by the huge M&M cutout which said "Forbes Top 200 Company". After three minutes of uneasy silence, the panel was kind enough to let us go. We deposited ourselves in the Chillsoc corner; as I sat down, I tried to make myself as small as possible.

"Did you see that! She danced with me!"

I decided it best not to point out to Scooby that she was dancing in a circle of babes & dudes and Scooby just happened to be the one adjacent to her.

We had proceeded straight from the campus to this nightclub in Gurgaon. As the War Room event ran longer than expected, we hadn't had the time to change and looked distinctly out of place in our business suits at the party (MSA formation party[1]).

After two hours of attempting to dance with almost every female that existed, Scooby accumulated us- me and Matar- in a corner. Shouting over the loud music he said, "You guys want to do something legendary?"

Matar shrugged. I asked "What?"

"Well, Bastard & I stole an entire crate of beer from the back."

I had no idea how he managed to do that. I thought I had had him in my sights the entire time.

"Let's get out, get drunk and have the night of our lives!"

"You tired of dancing with the babes *kya*, Scooby?" Matar shouted back.

Scooby straightened his tie and readjusted his suit before speaking. "Today was the start of something legendary. Team Kinetic Kids. The most legendary ass fucking in the history of mankind." He raised an imaginary glass to us. "So, I ask you, men, to drink- a crate of the finest stolen beer known to Gurgaon- to our shadiness. To our unabashed plagiarism. To our royal public fucking. May we stay a team forever and ever. And may we stay as stupid as we looked today." Scooby wiped an imaginary tear off his eye and bowed to imaginary applause.

Matar yelled "Yeah yeah all right. As a matter of fucking principle, I never say no to free booze anyway."

---

[1] Party to celebrate juniors joining MSA Societies

"Bing! Bing!"

"Matar... Um... Why are people pointing at us?" I wondered aloud.

"Matar man, did you know you are wearing a suit? You look so funny.... Oh wait! I am wearing a suit too! Matar man, did you know I am wearing a suit?" asked Bastard's voice happily.

I rubbed my eyes and found Bastard seated next to me, looking at everything around him with genuine childlike wonder in his eyes. I noticed that I was also wearing a suit. Also, wearing a suit was Scooby, crammed in between us, who was pointing with his index finger at every female he saw and making loud "Bing... Bing... Bing" noises.

"Hey Matar man, did you know that I have ten fingers? Ten! TEN!" Bastard continued holding up his hand to Matar in the front, in his happy trance.

"Bing... Bing... Bing... Bing. Challenger to Houston... Four more fertilized!"

"Stop doing that, Scooby! Wait... Matar, where are we? What is this thing? What... WHAT!" My voice got stuck in my throat, as my brain finally made sense of what my eyes had been beaming up to it for the past few minutes.

"Hey Matar man, do you know we are in a Rickshaw? A Rick... Shaw? Rick? Shaw?" Bastard was laughing madly now.

"BING! BING! BING! HOUSTON, THREE MORE DOWN!" Scooby yelled.

"Hey Matar man, did you know that you are driving the Rickshaw?"

Anna's coffee was as usual, too sweet. But the excess sugar helped take my mind off my pounding headache.

Bastard & Scooby were yet to graduate to a hangover; they were still officially drunk. Scooby was flirting lecherously with his coffee and ending every sentence he spoke with "Bing". Bastard was still in a state of gooey glee and *Did you know*'s.

"Matar, what happened dude?"

Matar sipped his coffee and looked at me with a sort of fatherly disappointment in his eyes. "We got drunk… last night. Given the state of these two, I don't think we should be attending the first class."

I looked at my watch and nodded. It was 9:50- well beyond historically permitted late entry times for the morning class anyway.

"Should we go somewhere quiet? Library- first floor? That's nearly always empty."

Matar nodded at my suggestion. Scooby got up, pointed theatrically to the sky and shouted, "Beam me up to the library, Scotty! Bing!"

It took us 20 minutes and 3 attempts to locate the perennially deserted first floor of the library. Bastard immediately fell asleep with his head on the table. Scooby was still Binging things, though with less fervor now.

"So, Matar, why were you driving a Rickshaw… a Rickshaw with us in it, this morning? Why is Bastard so happy? Why is… why is Scooby Binging? What happened last night?" I asked, looking over at the sleeping one and the Binging one.

Matar was reading the newspaper and took a minute to respond.

"You don't remember anything?"

"Nope... How come you remember... everything?" I asked.

Matar sighed. "Not everything... Some things. You really don't remember anything?"

I shrugged.

He folded the newspaper he had been reading & laid it on the table between us. "Okay... so here is what I remember of what happened last night. We did some very stupid things and I think Bastard is going to be less than happy when he wakes up... But fucking hell... this is one fucking hell of a story..."

Joker & the Thief & the Night

"To begin with an understatement, we got really drunk last night."

My pounding headache returned with a vengeance, giving a sort of thumping musical score background to Matar's story.

"And then we started driving around in Bastard's car."

"We drove around drunk?" I asked shocked.

"At the time it seemed a wise decision. Anyway, this was the very least of our stupidities. So, to continue- we started driving around in Bastard's 800. Initially, we were just shouting things out at people… a few fat uncles were called "fat"… some hot babes were called "hot" and so on. Scooby started it but we all joined in."

The musical score spread to the rest of my body with my hands, legs, knees- all thumping with the same ferocity as my head. Fuzzy images were surfacing in my head- mostly of shellshocked 'hot' females.

"So drunken driving, eve teasing… what law did we break next?" I inquired.

Matar ignored my query. "After the fourth bottle, Scooby started getting more & more baleful with every sip he took. He went on & on about how some girl keeps turning down his advances- slash-proposals."

"Who?" I asked, looking over at Scooby who was sleeping peacefully now.

"Don't know who... Someone he kept calling Big Bong."

"Oh..."

"Hari, so you fucking know? Who the fuck's Big Bong?"

"You don't know *kya* man? Really?"

Matar shrugged.

"It's Neelima. Scooby's had a thing for her for ages."

"Neelima... really?" A light dawned on Matar's face. He laughed. "Oh! How original! Bong because she's a Bong and Big because she's well... Big" Matar continued, still laughing, using his hands to make a gesture most women would have found demeaning.

"Wait a minute! Is that where Bing comes from? *Bi*g Bo*ng*?"

"Yeah... probably... Does make sense." Matar paused to digest the logic. "Anyway... so once his gloom receded a bit, Scooby decided that since he was handsome & sexy & powerful- after seven bottles of Heineken- he was going to Bing every female he came across... and not waste time with the niceties."

It was my turn to laugh. I regretted it as soon as I started... it made the thumping much worse.

"Meanwhile, Bastard was getting more & more cheerful with every sip. He went on & on about how beautiful the night was... how beautiful his steering wheel was... how beautiful Scooby was..."

"What was I doing?" I asked.

"You were in the backseat with me... You & I were um... mostly following Scooby's lead. I mean it was fun to be Scooby- to free oneself of oneself," Matar said smiling. "But after perhaps five or six bottles, you started speaking some gibberish which none of us could understand. Your sentences simply didn't make sense. Then all of us started shouting at you to shut up, which you eventually did."

"What was I saying?" I asked even as the words I had been speaking started reappearing in my head.

"Some fucking senseless bullshit... the words I caught- the ones you spoke most- were Meenakshi, God... And yeah the weirdest yet- August's Dorm. Who the fuck's August's Dorm?"

I shrugged barely concealing my smile. In my head, I smiled at August's monster sleeping peacefully in a corner.

Matar drank in a deep breath. "Somewhere in the midst of our monkey business, we got pulled over at some deserted junction by this solitary policeman on a bike. We must have called him something whilst Bastard was overtaking him. Scooby definitely did shout "*Pandu! Pandu! Bing! Bing!*" out at somebody but I am not really sure it was the same policewallah."

"What happened next?" I asked intrigued. An image of a bearded policeman with an impossibly large potbelly popped up in my head. A shard of broken memory told me he smelled of onions and tobacco.

Matar scratched his beard a bit before continuing, "Well, the *Pandu* read the riot act to us. He told us he would insert his lathi into our anuses & accommodate us in a deep dark dungeon made of shit, piss & blood. But of course, none of us were capable of any real worry anymore. We..." Matar started laughing abruptly.

"What did we do?"

"Well, Bastard started it. He remarked how beautiful the Pandu was, how beautiful his potbelly was, etc. etc. Scooby saw the walky attached to the Pandu's belt and remarked "*Sir, aapke paas to Walky Talky hai... Bahut mazza aata hoga.*" And then suddenly, without any warning, Bastard in a lightning fast move snatched the Walky from Mr. Pandu's belt."

"WHAT!"

"Yup... and then Bastard started running around shouting things into the Walky, with the fat Pandu huffing and puffing behind him. Things like "*Tango to Charlie*", "*Alpha to Delta*"... He was running in a circle and the Pandu ran behind him waving his lathi madly."

"What were the rest of us doing?"

"Well, we watched this madness for the first few rounds, then- we too started running after the Pandu. So, here we were in this bizarre game of chase the Pandu chasing Bastard with the Walky, shouting out suggestions like "*Roger That*" and "*Over & Out*"."

I could not help but laugh. By the time I stopped laughing, I had tears in my eyes and my nose, my fists hurt from thumping the table, my jaw hurt and my thumping also seemed to be laughing.

"So, what next?" I asked wiping a tear or two from my eyes.

"Well, I have no clue how long we ran... Maybe five minutes. Maybe thirty. But we stopped when the Walky suddenly cackled to life. Bastard nonchalantly tossed the Walky to the Pandu, who sat down on his haunches, breathing heavily.

'*Come in motherfucker*' said Walky Voice.

The Pandu managed a '*Haan bol*' into the Walky.

'*Where are you, motherfucker?*' Walky Voice asked.

'*ISBT intersection... I... have... four boys... drunk...*', our Mr.

Pandu replied, struggling for breath.

'*Fuck them... Proceed to Kashmere Gate... Jaspreet Walia has been spotted in that area*', the Walky ordered.

'*Walia... woh Chor?*'

'*Yes motherfucker.*'" Matar paused his narrative to scratch his back.

"Please tell me we came home after this" I pleaded.

Matar didn't reply. Instead, he unfolded the newspaper resting between us and pushed it towards me. He pointed to a headline which read "MASTER THIEF FOUND TIED TO TREE".

"Um... Did we do this?"

"Yup, we did. Only a few minutes after that joker Pandu left, Scooby spotted this shady character running in the distance. So of course, we ran up to him and accosted him."

"We accosted a Master Thief? Why?"

"Dunno... Maybe we felt guilty about screwing with that Pandu" Matar offered.

"So what did we do next?"

"Well Bastard held him in his grasp while the rest of us proceeded to interrogate Mr. Thief. You initiated proceedings by asking him '*Bhaiyya, kya aap Chor ho?*' A conversation ensued which I cannot recall. All I remember after that is us tying the thief to a nearby tree."

I proceeded to read the newspaper article, '*Dreaded Criminal... suspected involvement in 31 cases... one suspected murder... found with spectacles drawn around eyes with what seems to be black sketch pen... tied to hundred year old peepul tree... locals calling it a 'miracle'.*'

"We drew spectacles on the Master Thief's face?"

"Yeah after we tied him... I think it was you who said '*Chor chashma nahi pehnta.'"* So, Scooby rid him of his specs and drew them on his face."

"And where... where did we get the rope from?"

"Bastard's car. Anyway, then... then this happened..." Matar snatched the newspaper from me, folded it backwards and pushed it towards me.

The headline screamed "MARUTI 800 FOUND IN OPEN SEWER."

"We threw Bastard's car into the sewer! How? Why?"

Matar sighed. "Well, once we had tied that guy to the tree, we came back to the car. But it wouldn't start. Bastard got really pissed off. He kept going on and on about how the car was not beautiful anymore. So Scooby suggested let's bing it! So... we binged it! Into the sewer."

"How the hell did we manage to do this?" I asked looking incredulously at the picture of the semi- submerged car in the paper.

"The 800's a light car. Even kids can lift it. Anyway we were fucking drunk. We fucked around with a policeman. We caught a fucking master thief. That car was nothing in comparison."

I rubbed my eyes. Flashes of hitherto submerged memories were announcing themselves in my head, confirming Matar's story.

Matar cleared his throat. "Anyway, story's not finished yet. So, after chucking the car into the sewer, we walked around for a bit. Morning was beginning to break in. We came across this Rickshaw and Bastard remarked how cool it would be to drive a beautiful Rickshaw."

"We stole that Rickshaw!"

"Um... it was fucking unlocked dude- practically asking to be stolen. So... Bastard drove the Rickshaw while we sat in the back. After a while, I took over. We kept stopping at places and indulging in one idiocy after another. We peed in front of a shop. We definitely did fuck around with a stray dog... I think." Matar was scratching his forehead, straining hard to remember.

"Matar- my man? Why did you bring us straight to college? Why not take us home?"

"Because my dear Hari," began Matar, looking at his watch, "We have a fucking Economics test at 11."

Post the Economics test fiasco, I went to Deepak Bhaiyya's[1] room along with Matar, to collect some documents. An enterprising Delhi University employee had converted a PC into a TV in the corner of the room and an anchor in a suit and a weird beard, was narrating an incredibly improbable story.

Matar & I looked at the PC/ TV screen which flashed "*Kya ab kutte insaan se samajhdaar ho gaye hain?*"

We burst out laughing as Aaj Tak played visuals of a stray dog strolling around, looking studious & intelligent and wearing what were very clearly the Master Thief's spectacles.

[1] FMS Admin Employee

The Gas & the Game

The next day, still slightly hungover, we convened in the library after classes. The centre of our collective energies and attentions was the application form of a company that is (for some reason) one of the most sought after companies on every B-School campus, across the country.

There are few things as complicated, lengthy, terrible and feared in the world of an MBA as a TAS interview form. The TAS form is the longest form in the history of MBAkind. It will ask you everything- your blood group, your grades, your strengths- your weaknesses, your statement of purpose, your mission/ vision, short term/ long term goal, incidents in your life when you displayed leadership skills, bravery, creativity, problem solving ability, sexual prowess; father's blood group, grades, strengths... And so on. (*I exaggerate but only slightly.*) It is a form so terrible and complicated that mock forms were released, so that we could practice filling them.

"For problem solving ability, can I write I saved a babe from drowning in the river that runs by my house?"

"A fucking river runs by your house, Scooby?" Matar asked perplexed.

"Imaginary river. Imaginary babe. Try to keep up, Mats."

"What's with the river and the babe, Scooby?" I asked.

Bastard cleared his throat. "Scoob's mentor told him that TAS only selects people with social work on their forms/ CVs."

"So at least on the form and the CV, I am being very social" Scooby added.

Matar laughed. "Don't worry Scooby. You are plenty social."

We sat and discussed the answers for an hour or so. Scooby's incidents somehow always managed to involve a damsel in distress. Who was usually very hot. And who would generally sleep with him later to say 'Thanks'.

A few days latcr, I met Mowgli for CV perusal and general guidance along MBA's dimly lit pathways.

Mowgli went through my CV slowly. "Not bad. Not bad at all. Just remove that one... looks shady. And bold all the things I have underlined. You are mark-focused, right?"

In my head, Matar raised his hand and asked a FinSoc senior "Tell me in hindi... (sic) *Credit mein paisa andar gaya ke bahaar aaya*? And if *paisa bahar aaya*, then why the fuck are we writing 'To' with it and not 'From'?" I laughed at the memory, at the fact that I (or Matar) still did not know the answer to that question and replied "Mark- focused, of course."

Mowgli sighed. "Well, not a bad CV for FMCGs. Don't expect any consulting shortlists with your marks though."

"Don't expect. Don't want" I replied.

"You don't want that one lakh per month waali internship?" Mowgli asked puzzled.

Smiling I said "Naah, I would rather be a thousand times happier than paid ten times as much."

Mowgli laughed. "Achha, to more important things. Interview forms ho gaye? TAS done?"

"Haan, almost done. I am having trouble with creative problem solving waala question though. I don't remember having solved a problem creatively. Logically maybe, but never creatively."

"Arre, kiya hoga saale. Email your friends, relatives. Ask your mom. Or best, pick some incident from induction fortnight. A lot of shit happens in Induction. And once you find that incident, blow it out of proportion. Write it as if you were a bloody war hero or something."

I was mulling over Mowgli's latest, when I felt a hand on my shoulder. I looked up to find Matar who pointed to the wall-clock and said, "It's fucking time."

"Ab kya hai?" I asked agitated.

"FinSoc session. Cash Flow Discounting."

I sighed and slumped in my seat, before replying "Hope it's as much fun as it sounds."

"Mason Storm."

"Good one."

"Your turn."

"Monica Mattos."

"Ooh, vintage! S… S… Lemme see now… "

Bastard and Scooby were playing a game they had invented during a soporific session on tax law by an ancient prof from Law Faculty.

"Sarah Jay" Matar suggested.

"Yes! Sarah Jay! Go on Basty Boy."

"Doesn't count. Matar's not playing."

"Come on man. I am bored. 'Y' se bol."

"I am giving myself one point. And... Yasmine Bleeth."

"Yasmine Bleeth's not a pornstar! She's a Baywatch babe!"

Bastard laughed loudly. The FinSoc dude giving the ppt on Cash Flow Discounting paused and looked in our direction.

"Perhaps not in letter. But in spirit, yes" Bastard replied, after FinDude had resumed presenting the inedible indigestible bullshit. "Tell me, Scoob, haven't you ever..."

"Yeah yeah. I have. She counts. H... H... Lemme see now..."

After FinSoc let us off at around 10 in the night, we proceeded to the Domino's near campus, for a gastric celebration of Aastha's birthday. The entire original Udupi group was present. Bastard and an 8 by 8 female called Nishtha were the additions.

The game continued at the birthday shenanigans. To be fair to Scooby and Basty Boy, minus their game- the affair was fairly boring. Conversations were made mostly of flashes and clicks. Digicams & camera phones abounded and pictures of everything and anything were taken. To prove that fun was had. To prove that Aastha had had a birthday.

The four of us- the Kinetic Kids- sat in a huddle at the corner of a large rectangular table. Bastard led 32-28 from the afternoon. To make things interesting, Matar & I wagered on the competitors

(Matar on Scooby, me on Bastard). Names were articulated discreetly from the corner of mouths or sometimes, if too complicated, written down on napkins (carefully disposed off later). Amid pizzas, camera flashes and Mithun's "*Hey! Look at me!*" acts, nobody noticed the game going on in the corner.

In the end, Bastard won narrowly. 47-46. He won riding on a technicality that Scooby hadn't bet on. The winning name was of a male performer.

I made a hundred bucks. And learnt several interesting names.

As we stepped put and started our walk back to our residences, Matar & I fell in step with Aastha who quite innocently asked me "Hey, I overheard you guys discussing this Jenna Jameson at length. Who's Jenna Jameson?".

I was too shocked to reply. Matar, my wingman, however, shot back without missing a beat "She's this English woman who's recently set up this NBFC in the jungles of Chhatisgarh. To lend money to tribals."

"Wow. I didn't know that. Must be a great woman." An shadow of gloom clouded her face. "There's so much I don't know. You guys are so well prepared." She looked crestfallen at not knowing the name of an important businesswoman a few weeks before summer placements.

I doubled over laughing. Matar, who I could see was having trouble controlling his laughter too, shouted at the others. "He's having stomach ache! (*Suppressed Snigger*) Don't worry… he has them all the time. (*Escaped Snigger*) You guys, carry on. I'll take him to our PG."

After everybody else left, Matar & I sat on the pavement laughing for fifteen minutes.

Eight earthly revolutions of the sun later, August's testy tantrums gave way to September's mild manners. As September dawned, my life had come to revolve around application forms, GLs, classes, assignments, tests- the random nuisance of an average MBA day.

In September, I woke up to sleep deprivation. As I lived September, I was never sure what was real and what a dream. It was perhaps part of the reason why I had gone without thinking/ feeling for a week- why I had been the Monster to Meenakshi's love. I was becoming insomnia insane. I was Tyler Durden[1] .

Names of days didn't exist. Monday or Sunday was the same; if not lectures, we had MSA GL's. It was the worst in the Conclaves- the five or so conferences organized by each of the Soc's. Every Soc had a conclave- ranging from FinSoc to MarkSoc. We sat in the front rows (back rows occupied by seniors) gazing blankly into space- sleeping without sleeping- as guest speakers went on and on about gaseous goo like "*HR paradigms in the new millennium for the IT-SME landscape.*" After a while all I saw was the colors, all I heard was sounds; everything was incoherent.

Insomnia is not unlike August's monster. It is stronger, bigger and doesn't need emotions to feed on.

I awakened from my insomniac reverie to find that the old fat bald man, who was speaking 45 minutes ago, was still speaking. The seat beside me was empty- Matar had probably found a way to escape. I was just thinking about murdering Matar for not taking me with him, when he returned.

"You won't believe what just happened" he said.

---

[1] Fight Club

"What?" I asked.

"Here I was, fucking minding my own business, drinking water from that cooler thingy when I feel this tap on my shoulder. So I look around and see Swati looking at me with a question in her fucking eyes."

Swati was one of the 8 by 8 super-hotties. Scooby had rated her 9.90 on his scale. 0.10 points were deducted for what Scooby called 'Unnatural Asset Inflation.'

"She asked you out?" I asked chuckling.

"No. Much worse... Her eyes are red... almost fucking bloodshot. She leans towards me, so as to bring her face closer. There is Pritam nearby and two others- relatively deserted but still three people in sight. My first thought is she's gonna fucking kiss me. But then I notice her lips moving and then a whisper..."

Matar paused. He started toying with his turban, straightening it; then he proceeded to his beard, stroked it. The damn suspense was killing me.

"Ab bataega bhi?"

"Haan haan... So as you know she's wearing this yellow top, blue jeans..."

"I know what she's wearing!"

"And her usual push up bra... her boobs look big..."

"Matar. Bhenchod. What did she say?"

Matar cleared his throat loudly as the final step of his storytelling ritual. "So she leans over slightly and fucking whispers in my ear- *Where do you get your pot from?*"

"WHAT!"

Akshay, who was sleeping in the chair behind me, woke up to

my exclamation. The old man on the stage continued driveling on.

"So, what did you say?" I asked.

"Nothing. I fucking turned and ran. And told you the fucking story."

I laughed. "8 by 8 hotties asking you for pot! You have a sexy positioning man!"

Matar looked distinctly worried.

After the conclave got over, the second ConClub meeting (first one held immediately after the junior team was selected) was held around the ConClub desk in the MSA room. Suhaas- the President- spoke with a passion about how he wanted to make ConClub the hottest Soc in the MSA. To that effect, the first step (per Suhaas) was to have the most expensive party on campus and to steal the tag of the sexiest MSA Soc from the other Socs, which were described at length as the fuckers of various relatives.

And a handful of days later, with a week to go before summer placements, the party was eventually held at an insanely expensive lounge bar in South Delhi. I almost balked while looking at the menu. Among the cheapest dishes- a platter of "Chicken Rosinieri" (whatever that was) with "Serves two" written next to it- was for 900 bucks.

The bill, when it eventually came, was for approximately 32000. The next day, a pic of the bill was Suhaas' profile pic on Orkut. At a cost of 32000 (to the seniors), ConClub was sexy again.

O' Clouds Dark

It is perhaps a testament to Japanese engineering supremacy that Bastard's Maruti 800 still worked after being unceremoniously dumped in the sewer by us, on that fateful night. Initially the engine refused to start; but then (per Bastard) the mechanic gave the engine an almighty bang with an almighty wrench and it revived. Holding up his fingers with manic glee, Bastard said to us "Precision Engineering 0 – Brute Force 1."

I was thankful we had the car again, as with five odd days to go to summer placements, our lives involved a lot of running around. We had to get printouts of our CV's and other documents (from Patel Chest area in North Campus); passport size photos clicked and printed; suits bought or if pre-owned, dry-cleaned. Interview forms were being released by the hour and we had to rush to either submit or collect or photocopy.

Matar & I (finally) bought Kotlers and started to read them. Most nights, Scooby & Bastard joined us in our vision/ revision sessions.

Enriching discussions were held. I finally understood STP, 4P's etc. and also most of elementary finance. We made elaborate plans of thrashing FinSoc, once placements were over, for making it all sound so complicated.

With placements a day or two away, I invoked Mowgli one final time.

"See man, I got placed on Day 3. So I pretty much went through hell. Man, it sucks to see people around you getting placed. You begin to doubt yourself. Whether you are good enough or not." Mowgli's face was made of pain. "You feel like puking. You feel like not breathing."

"What if I don't get placed at all?" I asked.

Mowgli laughed. "Don't worry… It's FMS. You'll get placed. But learn from me. Never feel like shit. You made it to FMS. You are as good and as bad as everyone around you. Conversely, if you get placed on Day Zero, don't act like a star. Help people around you."

I nodded and wondered what fate held in store for me. Shitdom or stardom.

Later that day, the stars conspired to permit a final act of God before placements. In truth, it was more an act of Bastard than God. We were traveling in Bastard's car. Matar, Ruchi, Mithun and me- with Bastard driving.

I sat in the front with Bastard. Ruchi was rattling off some telecom sector facts mostly to the benefit of Mithun. I could see from Bastard's face that he was finding this irritating.

He finally spoke up. "Will you please shut up, Ruchi? If I hear the word ARPU again, I'll crash the car into a pole."

Ruchi ignored Bastard, gave him her I-am-a- woman-of-steel look in the rearview mirror and continued rattling off facts. "Ruchi, yaar, please. Can we just talk something fun? I really don't like to hear what all I don't know before placements." Matar too pleaded.

Mithun stepped in stammering. "Oye… ek to… ek to woh padha rahi hai… and… and… and…"

"Phone pe padh liyo, madarchod" Bastard cut him short.

An uneasy silence spread across the car. Ruchi broke the silence with "Take a right from here."

"Right? But your PG is straight ahead" Bastard replied.

"Haan I know. I have some work in Patel Chest. So take a right!" Ruchi shot back.

"Say 'Please'." Bastard retorted smiling.

Ruchi stayed silent.

Bastard stopped the car. He looked back and said slowly "Ruchi, don't fucking talk to me like I am your driver. Say 'Please'."

Ruchi stayed determinedly silent. Then as if she had been using the time to formulate a fitting response in her head, she said angrily "Say 'Please' to scum like you! Guys like you pay 8000 bucks to go out on a date with me! Treat me with some respect!"

"Enough. Get out, Ruchi" Bastard said calmly.

"What?" Ruchi looked shocked.

"I said get the fuck out of my car". Bastard's voice was (surprisingly) still calm.

Ruchi made a move as if to open her door. Matar stopped her. "No no he's kidding yaar. Basty, tell her you are kidding, yaar" Matar pleaded.

"No, Matar. Clearly, Queen Ruchi hasn't met enough guys like me. Ruchi… get out before I kick you out." There was a quiet anger building up in his voice.

Ruchi got out and banged her door shut. Mithun got out too and followed her shouting/ stammering "No! No! R… R… Ruchi stop!"

"Anybody else wants to leave?" Bastard asked.

Matar sighing said "No". I shook my head.

Bastard started the engine again and we drove off.

The campus was a buzz of activity as summer placements lurked just around the corner. Walls were repainted, curtains changed, rooms vacated & cleaned. Soc's started giving us final revision lectures. Teachers eased up on assignments/ tests.

Everybody was in a collective state of anxiety. Everybody held their breaths. Beyond the campus, the sky turned murky and grey. But it did not rain.

Then Came the Merrymakers

Memory is a strange thing. You can have the night of your life & forget about it and not forget one single detail of something else. Like the first day, there was an ant in Matar's beard. Like the taste of food on each and every day. Like the little things which became big things later. Like the smell of weird on Bastard. Like watching this Deepika Padukone movie on my laptop, whose songs continue to evoke strange emotions in me. Emotions that could fill a cheap bread roll.

Before it all began, the PlaceCom addressed us one final time. Their tone was mellower than it had ever been. Madhavan spoke in a tone that was firm without being rude. He asked us to stay together as a batch. To not celebrate or applaud our or our friends' placements till the very last guy was placed.

It was an experience. It was jubilation, dejection, anxiety, nervous sweat, anger, bitterness and more- all mixed together hurriedly to fill one of Anna's bread rolls. I will never forget the smells, sounds, sights and feels of the time- everything is so vividly etched in my mind that I can, at any time, open the door in my head and step into the room again- that fateful room made of a hundred odd pretenders.

At every B- School across the country, they call the first day- Day Zero. It's a very MBA way of counting.

Business suits make you look good. People who look good in normal clothes, look even better. MBAkinds (probably) wear suits beçause it is difficult to say 'No' to a beggar in a suit. Sure he knows nothing, but at least his tie is top notch.

Bastard was the first of the Kinetic Kids to get placed. He was, in fact, probably the first person on campus to get placed. He got through a consulting firm whose process had begun (& ended) pre Day Zero. (When Bastard's result was announced, Mithun uttered a loud "Boo".)

The zeroth day, there were very few companies. Such companies were called 'Dream Companies'. It was everybody's dream to get into these companies. To get that prestigious name on their CVs. To get in and jostle for a PPO.

I got no shortlists at all on Day Zero. The Dream Companies asked me to "Dream On". I sat and watched people around me getting placed. As the day came to an end, I flicked an ant out of Matar's beard.

Fifteen people were placed on Day Zero.

Day One began with sandwiches and tea.

"Today is my day, lads. I can feel it in me bones... Gharrrrrr" said Scooby in what was supposed to be an imitation of Davy Jones.

Matar shrugged. I said, "Hope I at least get some shortlists today. At least you guys had shortlists yesterday. I was so bored."

"You were better off" Matar replied. "It sucks not getting placed after having an hour long interview. Which went decently well."

I did not know what to say to that. I just ate my sandwich in silence.

I saw my first shortlist on Day One evening. A bank had shortlisted me (probably by mistake) for their process. The first round was a GD based on a three page case provided to us. My brain went to sleep one paragraph into the case. It was boring, verbose and laden with data. The case ended to five questions which we had to address in fifteen minutes.

The discussion that ensued was as boring and lifeless as the case itself. The participants showed life only in cutting each other and capturing air time; but once they had the group's attention, they floundered, blundered, meandered. I managed to get in two- three times and plant a kick on the discussion football being kicked around. By the end of the GD, only two of the five questions had been addressed somewhat and the company representative observing us seemed to not be listening to the '*I beg to differ*'s or '*I would like to add here*'s or the hundred or so catchphrases that are taught at coaching institutes across the country.

The only highlight of the GD was when Austin cut off Mithun in the dying minutes of the GD. Agitated, Mithun shot back "Hey! L... Let me finish my point!" To which Austin famously replied, "Let me finish it for you."

As Day One ended, PlaceCom stood facing us as they had the previous day. Madhavan spoke in a gentle voice. "So I am going to announce the results of today. Like yesterday, nobody claps or cheers anybody."

The names were reads off a list that Madhavan carried. As I had no interview calls at all, I wasn't expecting anything for myself. Just looking forward to going home and crashing.

And then amid the clouds dark were two happy drops of rain. Matar & Scooby found their names on Madhavan's list. Davy Jones said "Gharrrr!" with one eye (under invisible eye patch) closed for effect. Matar, on the other hand, refused to react to my congratulatory pat.

Later, Bastard dropped me and Matar home.

As I lay in my bed, Matar said gently "Don't you worry man. Tomorrow's gonna be your day. Fucking busiest day of summers tomorrow."

I smiled and assured him that I was not worried even though Worry sat on my brows. At 2 in the night I received a message from Meenakshi. "How's it going? Any luck yet?" it asked.

The Worry on my brow paralyzed my fingers. I switched my mobile off, pushed it under my pillow and tried to go back to sleep.

Matar was already dressed up when my alarm rang. I noticed he was writing something.

"Hi love! Good morning! Extended your alarm time by fifteen minutes. Hope you don't mind."

"What you writing Matar?" I asked, stifling a yawn.

"One of your fucking forms for today. Lengthiest one yet since TAS" he replied. "Chal naha le. Bastard will be here in 15 minutes."

I looked at our alarm clock. It was 6:15.

Day Two. At college, before the drama for the day began, there was breakfast again. This time it was McDonald's fare with Iced Tea.

Scooby was reading the day's news to me off ET. He paused to ask "Abey so raha hai kya?"

I opened my eyes and replied "No Scooby. Go on... I am listening. The headache's just getting bigger and bigger. It's probably my sinus."

Bastard, who I thought had been sleeping, sat up suddenly. He fished something out of his suit's chest pocket- something that looked like an opaque flask with exotic inscriptions right out of Harry Potter. He then opened up the contraption and poured several drops of it into my tea.

"Polyjuice Potion?" I wondered.

"Poly what?" Bastard asked clearly confused. "It's Vodka dude. Good for your nose thing."

I laughed and gulped down my spiked drink. I felt better almost instantly. In my head, I pictured the drink landing a Bastard style punch on my sinusitis.

I looked up to find Bastard snatching the day's ET off Scooby. "Look, Hari, this shit is not going to get you placed. Just sit back and relax for now. Let luck take its course. These two idiots had five odd shortlists before they converted. You have only had one."

Matar looked up from the third form of the day he had been filling for me, perhaps to respond to being labeled an idiot. However he then thought better of it.

"Hey, have you citizens noticed the Khulla group?" Scooby asked.

We had. Everybody had. The Khulla group, called so because their unofficial leader- Gagan- had a tendency to keep his mouth open at all times, had been the most vocal group in the room since summer placements started. The Khullas saw & magnified rivalries where they didn't exist, quarrels & tiffs which hadn't happened (or if they had, were trivial in nature) and defended each other fiercely on issues as inconsequential as hairstyles or answers given in HR class (Eg. "*No, sir. I disagree with you; I think Gagan is right.*") To them, everybody and everything was in camps; to them, FMS was a battlezone and it was their camp vs. the world.

The Khullas believed they were the FMS elite. And they almost were. They had weighty CV's. Several of them were in the top 14 from the entrance exam. Most of them held plum society posts- two of them, PlaceCom positions. And since placements started, they had been cheering quite lustily each and every one of their members' placements (despite Madhavan's repeated warnings) and jeering those of people from what they saw as rival camps.

Placements being an emotional and taxing time for everybody, Madhavan hadn't shouted at the Khullas outright but just taken Gagan aside and tried to reason with him. He had also made several indirect references/ pleas/ minor threats to shut the Khullas up. But to no avail.

Bastard cracked his knuckles. "Wait till you get placed Hari. I am gonna..." He let the sounds of his fist joints cracking into place complete the sentence for him.

My first shortlist of the day was an FMCG major. The GD was case based again with the case being that of a fictional FMCG firm looking to launch a herbal toothpaste. We had to decide on the media plan and the 4P's[1] for the product.

The discussion football (again) began being kicked around with no sight of any side scoring. Cleverer from my first GD experience, I

[1]A marketing framework

decided to take a different tack. I deflated the ball.

I interrupted Aastha who had been mentioning something about rural distribution. "Aastha, if I may interrupt... The past few minutes, we have been discussing the launch plan for this product in rural areas. But come to think of it- why would a villager buy a herbal toothpaste that is priced higher than a Colgate or a Pepsodent? Wouldn't he rather use his *datun* stick?"

I paused to collect my thoughts but to my surprise, nobody exploited my stoppage. So I stepped on the gas. I talked of urban distribution, media planning, 4P's. People started to follow my lead. Even though I got very few opportunities to enter the GD again, my name kept coming up in the clichéd catchphrases of yore ("*As Hari said...*" or "*Taking Hari's point forward...*"). As the GD ended and we trudged back to our room, I grew confident of getting an interview call from the company.

Sure enough I did. The panel focused on personal questions which I did decently well on. The only low point of the interview was that I floundered on the question of what I wanted to do with my life. I told the panel that in the long run, the one thing I wanted to do most in life was to write stories and see them published. On their insistence, I took them through the story which I had been writing since the day of my interview- the story that had come to me in a dream (a daydream to be specific).

The youngest of the interviewers- a tall dashing bald 40 something then asked me, "So what's a writer- a poet like you doing in a B-school?"

I did not know the answer to this. To be fair, I had been asking myself the same question over and over, through my life. What am I doing in Science Section? What am I doing in an engineering college?

What am I doing at ABC? What am I doing in FMS?

And perhaps to my detriment, I let Hari- the poet answer instead of Hari- the desperate-for-a-placement B-School student. "Honestly sir, I have been asking myself the same question."

The baldie smiled and said. "Whether you make it or not, Hari, I will remember you." And just as I was at the door- about to exit- he said, "Finish your story, Hari. Screw everything else." I smiled back at him, nodded and left.

I had barely taken my seat, when my name was called again. "Hari Parmeshwar. Blue Zone Consultingl!"

Matar straightened my tie and brushed something off my suit and I was off again. This time, the company was a consulting firm that had been set up by an FMS alumnus.

The first interview being largely finance, didn't go too well. However, to my own surprise I managed to proceed to the next round, where I was interviewed by senior management. The panel in this round, focused more on my work experience than my limited knowledge of finance. And this time to the question of long term goals, I managed to make up some gas about "Learning and facing knew challenges as I climb up the corporate ladder."

Lunch was being served when I returned. Scooby was in the process of claiming more than his fair share of lunch. (He was stacking pizza boxes under his chair- four had already been stacked when I entered.) Matar & Bastard were helping someone with an online test.

"Hiya! How did it go?" Matar asked when he noticed me but then held up a hand to silence me as soon as I started to speak. "Wait... Give us five minutes."

As I sat down and narrated the tales of my two interviews, whilst gorging on pizzas (Scooby had managed to corner five boxes- we had eight boxes amongst us) I realized that the interviews had gone better than I thought they had. I had managed to answer every question, even the fin ones. I hoped that I got through- that the circle of nervousness, jealousy and bitterness ended for me.

Through the day I received no more calls. Even though Bastard's logic (that I had made it to one of my interviewee firms and my CV had thus, been pulled by the PlaceCom from the others for the day) made sense, my sinuses reacted, my tummy grumbled with nervous anxiety and my eyes burned. I waited with bated breath for Madhavan's appearance and the results of the day.

At 12:30 AM, the PlaceCom appeared. Madhavan held his usual printout in his hand and spoke softly. "Okay, guys. Results for the day. As always, no clapping or cheering." He looked deliberately in the direction of the Khullas.

"Preeti Gulati. TMT Finance."

And with that, all the Khullas had been placed. They erupted into a loud sustained applause- their loudest yet. Parallely, boos started emanating from different corners of the room. "GUYS! CALM DOWN! CALM DOWN!" Madhavan shouted in his sternest possible voice.

The noise died down. "If I see anybody cheering or booing, I will personally screw his or her happiness. DO I MAKE MYSELF CLEAR?"

The room became nods and whimpered 'Yes'es.

"Hari Parmeshwar. Blue Zone."

It felt as if I had dissolved to nothing. I felt nothing- not relief, not jubilation, not Matar or Scooby or Bastard's pats or handshakes.

I was in a daze as Madhavan announced the rest of the names, as we later walked home to our PG, as I called up Meenakshi (who didn't pick up)- then messaged her, as I went to sleep.

The next morning, I felt almost the same. The newborn sun danced its rays off clouds but was ignored. Birds tweeted merrily and were ignored the same by the perpetual romantic on the rooftop. I felt happiness at my peripheries but not in my heart. But as the clouds parted and the sunrays started to dance on my fingers, my railing, I felt an odd sense of relief- a feeling of truce- bereft of any joy.

Day Three, I sat and ate and drank. I filled forms for others; shared whatever little gyaan I had with some. I watched this Deepika Padukone movie on my laptop. Played Pocket Tanks[2] with Matar. Then Scooby.

In the evening over hot coffee, we discussed stuff. Discussed life. Love. Raindrops.

"I remember when I was small, in first standard, this one day it rained."

Bastard had just started adding Vodka to his coffee. "Want some, HP? No? Um… You were saying?"

I sighed. "I was five. This one day exams had just ended. And as we stepped out of the school, it started to rain."

I paused to take a sip.

"It was the happiest day of my life. Everything felt happy. The raindrops on my skin. The color of the world. The cool breeze. The smell of earth."

"What you saying HP?" Matar asked.

---

[2]A computer game

"I am saying nothing has ever felt as good- as happy as that day. I know I will never love anything as much as I loved raindrops as a kid."

And that thought became the fifth guy in our midst. It sat with us and watched us as we sipped our coffees in silence; it took potshots at our heads and made us wonder what we were doing, what we really wanted in life.

That evening, the PlaceCom assembled in front of us. So did forty odd seniors who had been handling the placement logistics. Everybody was smiles and cheer; a cake and a champagne bottle had made their way to the head of the room- but no one spoke a word. With a smile on his face, Madhavan started reading names off his customary list. And after he had spoken the last name, he shouted "And with that, the batch is placed!"

The entire room erupted into wild celebrations. The cake was taken apart and smeared around. Scooby found his way to the champagne bottle and began drenching everyone in sight with champagne. Each of the male PlaceComies was either given bumps or some parallel form of physical reverence. Amid the commotion and the confusion, nobody noticed Bastard punching Gagan savagely in the face. (Gagan was later found passed out in a corner. He was quite confounded when he came to and believed that it was the champagne cork that had hit him.)

As we stepped out of the room, out into the dying light of the day, the skies uttered a loud exclamation. As it started to rain, I turned my face up to the sky to let raindrops kiss my face.

'You know, man, there are less violent ways of getting things done,' said Nimai, [illegible] dripping from the corner of his mouth.

City of Many Joys II

The cat that lived in Anna's food cupboard was out on her rounds and was currently, pawing at Matar's packed suitcase. Bastard's kick met her in the belly and she flew about a foot, screaming hysterically.

"You know, man, there are less violent ways of getting things done" said Matar, curd dripping from the corner of his mouth.

Bastard laughed his mad laugh. The cat sat herself atop the quivering plastic table opposite us, giving us dirty looks.

It was the day after summer placements. The campus was empty except for Anna, a few Profs, the four of us and Anna's cat. Almost everybody had gone home for the ten odd days long vacations. Sunlight filtered through the gaudy green plastic rooftop that Anna's had, which let both sunlight and rain in. The plastic made the sun look green & giddy and it was easy to be cheerful when the sun was so green & gaudy & giddy.

"Hey do you guys know StanChart is really pissed with FMS?" Scooby asked.

A week ago, we would have cared but now with everything being so green & giddy & peaceful, it was difficult to worry.

Five or so bites later, Matar eventually asked "Why the fuck?"

"Well, first, everybody kept getting confused between the banks. People spoke of Citi's products in StanChart interview, StanChart's products in HSBC interview and so on. But the tipping point for StanChart was Aastha."

"What she do?" I asked in the tone in which Shaggy often said "Scooby Dooby Doo".

The nuance was lost on Scooby who retorted, "During her interview, she said that her aim in life was to be like Jenna Jameson."

"WHAT!" Droplets of curd flew out in different directions.

"You know, Matar" started Bastard laughing, wiping curd droplets off his face, "there are less violent ways of exclaiming."

"Sorry bossman." Matar sighed. "This is all our fault. We should have never played that game at her birthday."

Bastard was having trouble controlling his laughter- he was rolling from side to side, thumping everything in sight- hands on belly- struggling for breath. "She really said that?" I asked, wary of Bastard's thumps getting closer & closer to my plate of rice.

Scooby nodded his all knowing nod. Bastard managed to utter "Stupid bitch" before proceeding to thump the table with more vigor than ever and flick laughter tears out his eyes. The sun was green & giddy and it was impossible to feel guilty. The rest of us too started to laugh.

There was mocking laughter in her eyes. "Sir, may I help you?" she asked nonchalantly, without really wanting to help me.

I didn't think she could, in any case. I stood and stared at the fare board for the airline which had dressed her in radiant red- made her look like a bogus Barbie. I repeated her question in my head, to myself. "Hari, how can I help you?"

I stood staring at the board for a long time, unable to help myself. I did not want to go to the house of my birth- the place that had made me the science student, the engineer, the IT employee and finally the MBA; the place where my romanticism was born as an escape from Mother's unabated expectations and Father's stoic indifference. Even though I had lived there more than twenty years of my life, I had hardly any happy memories there.

But then, go to Kolkata? Mother *expected* me to come home. (She had spoken of some business of me being shown around in social circles- so that it was easier to get me married off, once I had a job post- FMS.) Besides, I had no place to stay in Kolkata; I had lived in rented accommodation arranged by ABC.

And then, I behaved as any addict would. Perhaps, the weeks I spent in Delhi's polluted air had dulled my senses; otherwise I would have made the decision in a matter of seconds. Bogus Barbie swiped my credit card and printed me a ticket.

Kolkata was hotter than I remembered. But I felt at ease, at home. I roamed around listlessly, drinking in the hot air. I wandered with no aim, taking one bus after the other, walking cramped streets.

She had not taken my calls since the day I got placed except once, to tell me that she was quite busy with some family function. I thought of her as I wandered. She had been different since the day we made love- her music was changed and had less cheer. Her messages were crisper; our conversations were shorter. I hoped that now that I was here, all that would change. I hoped that it had always been that way, that I was only noticing now- making a mountain of a molehill.

By a queer twist of fate, the last bus I took for the day dropped me a street off from where I was putting up. Anirban, my old landlord, had rented me a dilapidated old attic on his roof, for seven days.

On the fifth day of Kolkata, we finally met. She wore a white saree with resplendent red borders- something Bengali women wear. (Unlike me, Kolkata was her real home.) She looked different- older, wiser, mature. There was a worry line etched in her forehead and when she spoke or opened her mouth, a tributary arose from it to her cheek.

It must be because I am a poet that I noticed. As poets, we are blessed/ cursed to notice everything- we notice the fourteen different shades of blue the sky is, the hues of red on a rose, the smell of raindrop kissed earth- things that every other specie of human takes for granted.

I noticed her worry tributary, that her hands shook, that her lips quivered slightly when she spoke, that her eyes were a hue of rose red, that her eyelids were heavier and weighed down. And I understood.

When she asked me about placements, I took her hand in mine and kissed it. I closed my eyes, held her hand to my nose and breathed her unique Meenakshi smell. When I opened my eyes, I noticed that she was smiling for the first time since we met.

I was energized by her smile. I took her by the hand, led her out the restaurant. When she asked "Where to?" I told her I didn't know. She gave in to my madness- we walked hand in hand till I grew tired of running away and sat down on a bench.

She sat down silently beside me, looking away- looking at a mockingbird mimicking a telephone ring in a nearby tree. I pressed her hand hard and she looked at me, her eyes asking me the question that her lips weren't.

"Meena" I sighed. "I am sorry about that day... I wasn't really myself." Wind blew a leaf into my hair. She picked it out.

"I know I hurt you, Meena. But... I love you. You are the only thing in my life that I treasure; the only piece of the illogical puzzle that makes any sense."

Her eyes met mine as I said this. I saw that she was trying to smile, trying to say something as she smiled, trying to fight back tears while she wanted to say something and smile. In the end, her tears won.

I took her in my arms and kissed her forehead. She put her head on my shoulder and closer her eyes. As she cried quietly on my shoulder and the mockingbird mocked telephones, I too started to cry.

It was evening when she let go. She was still finding it difficult to speak; tears would emerge faster than her words could. She finally managed to say "Hari... I... have to go."

I held her in a tight hug and kissed her tears. "I love you, Meenakshi. I would rather always be with you than anybody anywhere."

"Then be with me, Hari" she said quietly.

My heart broke from the pain in her voice. I did not know what to say to that. I sighed in pain and said softly "I promise we'll be together forever... once I am done with Delhi."

She looked as if she wanted to say something but then, she held back. She wiped her tears on a tissue, restored her goddess grace to her face and got up. "Bye Hari. Stay in touch." Her sad smile broke the pieces of my heart further.

I saw her walk away. The sun setting ahead of her, gave her a fiery aura and she looked more like Durga than any idol could. I sat on the bench for hours, in more pain than I had ever been.

All my life, I have never seen the sun look that beautiful or that pink ever again. I call the sun of that day- the 'Sun of Meenakshi's Sorrow'.

My memory of the rest of Kolkata is hazy. I do not recall much between her walking away from me and Delhi walking back into my life.

The Kid We Barely Knew

"Ceterus Paribus" Bastard declared. Attar Singh looked at him bewildered and wordlessly handed him the parantha with butter on top, as requested.

I was back in Delhi, at one of FMS' favorite night-time eating joints. It was a rather dark night. The pollution meant that the sun or the stars or the moon were hardly ever visible here.

Scooby waved his parantha bite/ imaginary wand at Matar. "Ceterus Paribus!" he yelled. "Right out of Harry Potter it is!"

"Who the fuck's Citrus Papyrus?" Matar asked.

"Mats, Economics! Padha nai kya?" Scooby retorted.

"Nope… Matar & I have done Linear Prog till now" I replied.

"And HR" Matar added.

"Who does HR more than a day before exams!" Scooby exclaimed.

"Have you fucking seen previous year papers, Scooby? All kinds of weird theories and laws asked in HR man. Woh chhod… Basty, explain your love for this Cetrus Pabyrus."

Bastard swallowed the bite he had been savoring thoughtfully and took a swig from his pocket flask. "Ceterus Paribus means 'All other things being the same'. You should know this. ET[1] often uses this expression."

"Don't buy, don't read" Matar responded.

Bastard burped crudely before proceeding "So for instance, all other things being the same would you rather have 8 pack abs or not?"

"What do you mean by all other things being the same?" Matar asked.

"It means you wake up one morning to find you have 8 pack abs. Everything else is the same. You haven't spent thousands of bucks in a gym or had to sweat for it. Everything else stays same; only you have abs now."

Matar pinched his slight bulge before replying "Yeah why not."

Bastard continued "So apply this to everything in your lives. Ceterus Paribus would you like to marry a rich girl or poor? Both love you the same, both are equally attractive…"

"Ceterus Paribus would you marry a girl with big boobs or small?" Scooby added.

Three Khullas who happened to be passing by, looked at us weird. Bastard shrugged off Scooby's corollary and went on "It makes life infinitely simple. Come to think of it guys, Ceterus Paribus is probably why are doing MBAs. Because all career options were equivalent to us and we simply took the one with the highest paying potential."

"Fucking profound" Matar replied.

"Of course, the truth is" Bastard said "it never really works- ceterus paribus. Life has too many variables."

---

[1]Economic Times

In the distance, Attar Singh nodded as if he understood.

Amid life's many variables, we changed. Something had passed between us that day of the mockingbird. She was now no longer worried if I spent time with other females, no longer suspicious or jealous; we talked/ messaged less and when we did, we traded silences more. But it was a quiet understanding silence- a sound of two breaths in love who just liked to hear the other. Amid life's variables and love's tumult, we were changing- becoming constant- unhurried, unworried lovers.

And this was a constant unvarying thought in my head as I stepped into my first Semester exams at FMS. It calmed me- helped me focus. As people around me were stumbling on the mysteries of Statistics, Linear Programming, Economics or Accounting, I held the conversations I didn't have with Meenakshi with abstruse texts. I read and practiced and read some more. In ten odd days, I was quite well prepared- I knew things I had never known and Scooby/ Matar were beginning to refer to me as 'Ghissu'.

There was always a subculture of spamming at FMS but amid the tensions of exams, it took to dizzying heights. If there was something happening under the FMS sun, it was spammed across. Several times, important notification mails or email attachments got lost in the sea of spams and were discovered only once the relevant exam was over. Major points of email discussion were disappearing Economists (from the MSA room), a lost laptop, the coin shaped black mark around Gagan's right eye, 99's evergreen love for 64, Supercommando Dhruv/ Nagraj, storylines of Bhojpuri movies, quoted dialogues from such classics as 'Gunda', 'Mardon Waali Baat', 'Paap ko jalaa ke rakh kar dunga', etc. Perhaps absorbed in thoughts of photocopying class notes or buying course books, people began leaving their email accounts open on computers in the CC or their laptops unattended in the MSA room, which resulted in mails such as "I am feeling reaaaaal horny... Help!" being sent across to the entire batch, from their ids (by someone who chanced across a logged in email id).

Exams at FMS were mean devils, contrary to our expectations. None of the teachers set a paper with any choices in it. This meant that you left syllabus portions at your own peril because sometimes a certain portion would have a game- changing disproportionate weightage assigned to it in the paper. The questions were usually tough; case studies long; I struggled to attempt my papers within three hours.

Bastard on the other hand, somehow contrived to consistently leave the exam hall within two hours (of the allotted three), every exam. At the end of every exam, we would sit at Anna's and consume egg-Maggi. Matar & Scooby would (usually) begin to discuss the paper which Bastard would (usually) soon forbid (unless he was reclined comfortably with his eyes closed or far far away lost in his thoughts). We would then end up in Bastard's 800, head home and prepare for the next paper.

Matar & I were walking to college for our first lecture post exams, when I heard a loud guttural sound originate behind me. I turned and saw Tom Cruise in the distance, riding his black mean ode to masculinity towards us. He wore a suit & tie, a helmet made of testosterone and black biking gloves. Somewhere, U2 was playing the Mission Impossible theme.

Matar picked his phone and U2 stopped playing. Tom Cruise slid his bike to a stop near me (popping a rear tyre wheelie as he did so), at FMS gates and took off his helmet. It took me a second to recognize him behind his shades.

"You!"

Bastard grinned. "Just got her from Bombay. We've never been apart this long."

Matar's phone was saying "Hello! Hello?" as he stared at Bastard openmouthed.

"Bike! Phadoo! Sexy!" I exclaimed, my mind unable to forge complete sentences yet.

Bastard smiled. "Couldn't bring her here right away 'coz she was being repaired." He patted the fuel tank lovingly. "She was in an accident."

"Fuck fuck fucking fuck fuck!" articulated Matar who had recovered from shock. He moved on to other swearwords, then to synonyms of those swearwords.

Bastard laughed. Amid the swearstorm I said "Class first! Sem two! Late!"

Bastard parked his bike and we went to class together; Matar walked slightly behind us exhausting his dictionary of swearwords.

"What did you do with the 800?" Scooby asked.

We stood in a circle of admirers around Bastard's Honda, after the first class. The admirers were forbidden to touch her, stare at her for greater than ten seconds or refer to her as an inanimate object. (The Honda was clearly a 'she'.) A note was pasted beneath the plate that said "BL8C-221B" with all of Bastard's Honda laws printed on them.

"Still got the Maruti" Bastard said. "You guys can have it if you want" he declared to Matar & me.

"Why the suit man?" I asked, looking away from the bike fearful of violating the ten second rule.

"Got to go somewhere after classes" he replied.

"Areva?" Scooby inquired.

Bastard looked bewildered. "Areva what?"

"The live project interview" Scooby explained. And then, realizing something, he continued "Wait… Your name wasn't in yesterday's PlaceCom mail. I don't recall any name starting with a 'B'."

"You know Scooby, Bastard isn't my real name" he said laughing. "Anyway, not that LP[2] bullshit. Somewhere else."

The second lecture of Sem Two was bunked to unravel Bastard's mysteries and devour glucose biscuits & tea.

"No Mats, I am not getting married." He turned to me. "HP, I am not going for an off campus internship interview- I am quite happy with my summers firm." And then to Scooby. "And Scoob, no, I am not wearing the suit because it goes with the bike." Bastard paused to sip his vodka spiked tea.

Matar & I fought over the last Parle-G before deciding to halve it.

"I have to go to my graduation college today. Some function…"

"Your fucking engineering college was in Delhi?" Matar asked.

"No Matman. My fucking *college* was in Delhi" Bastard replied.

---

[2]Live Project

"Wait. WAIT!" Scooby said. "So, you… you're telling me you're not an engineer?"

"Yup" Bastard said.

Scooby's voice quivered with emotion as he spoke. "That changes everything. Everything. Every. Thing."

"What does that change?" Bastard asked.

"Everything!" Scooby banged the table to emphasize his point and held his forehead in his hands. He recovered to ask "If you're not an… an engineer, then what are you?"

"I thought you guys knew." He sipped his drink noisily before- "I am a doctor."

"WHAT!" Scooby yelled. Matar swore. I spilled the sip I was to take onto my T-shirt.

"You… you… are… a PhD?" asked Scooby, holding his fingers to his eyes.

"A doc of the medical kind, Scoobster" the doctor corrected him.

Scooby got up suddenly. "I have to go!" he declared. "Could you excuse me… DOCTOR!"

"Sure" said Bastard, pushing his chair forward good humouredly.

Scooby, however, just stood there, hands on hips. "What else do we not know about you? You a convict? Serial killer? You (*cough cough)* married? With kids?" His voice quivered wildly as he asked savagely "What… Who are you?"

Bastard sighed. "It ain't my fault you guys weren't listening during the induction intros. Or that you clowns didn't take a look at my CV at all."

Matar cleared his throat. "If you are the batch's only doc, how come nobody comes up to you for... for medical advice? Or for that matter, talks about it?"

Bastard settled into his seat deeper, the back of his head comfortably nestled in his palms. "Dunno, Mathead. But I like it this way."

Scooby sat down. For several minutes, we sat in silence digesting Bastard's secret and Anna's tea.

"Wait a minute!" Scooby exclaimed. "If you are a medical grad from Delhi, what was your bike doing in Mumbai?"

Bastard leaned back & shrugged.

"You live in Bombay?" Scooby offered. Bastard shook his head 'no'.

A few seconds later and then Matar- "Work ex in Bombay?"

Smiling, Bastard made a lazy tick mark in the air with his index finger.

In the evening, Scooby & I were playing a version of ping pong we had just developed (which did not necessitate the use of the ping pong table) when Matar appeared panting, sweating.

"Have... you... guys... fucking... checked... E... mail?" he asked amid gasps of breath.

"No darling. You left us here playing TT, remember?" Scooby alleged.

"Where... is... Doc?"

"Bastard left ten minutes ago" I replied.

"Come... CC... Email...Fucking scandal."

It was quite a fucking scandal. Somebody going by the name of Anguished.FMS.Student@gmail.com had emailed the batches and the entire faculty (with proofs attached) about an apparent breach of power by the General Secretary, Anand. Apparently, Anand had abused his post to get himself a shortlist in a national level event. Anand shot back stating he was innocent, that the proofs were forged. A GBM (General Body Meeting) of the seniors was held (with first years not invited) wherein Anand offered his resignation and the seniors accepted. Just as we were coming to terms with this unique circus, within two days of Anand leaving his email account open (by accident) on a laptop in the MSA room and Anguished.FMS.Student mailing across whatever he found in Anand's id, we had a new Gen Secy in place.

Calories, Brothers & The Other Feline

Come mid November, Delhi's winter was yet an infant and his tantrums were muted. He howled in the mornings and nights; covered everything he could find with mist & dew- rent the air with his fog. But in the afternoons, he would forget who he was and Delhi would be as hot as summer.

"You know, you guys could have just fucking raced bikes or done palm wrestling or something."

Bastard didn't react. Scooby said "Ah, but this is infinitely more fun. Just look at the faces of people around us."

Dressed in our FMS sweats, we were pretty much the centre of attention. We had been getting odd looks all morning.

Scooby chuckled. "Do you know that aside from us, fifteen other FMSites are giving CAT?"

"Why the fuck?" Matar asked.

"Because everybody still wants Ahmedabad" Scooby retorted.

"Fucking Ahmedabad. Bloody IIM-A sneezes and the papers report it on first page. And we bloody get pneumonia and they don't want to fucking hear about it" said Matar passionately.

"Matar, quit whining about your Soc's troubles" Scooby reacted.

Matar sighed. "My point is they aren't fucking better than us. Only fucking better known."

"So what are the terms of the bet?" I asked changing the topic.

"It's an intricate bet." Scooby fished out a paper & pen and started to draw circles and arrows and began to explain. At the end of five minutes and after several circles & arrows & formulae had been imbibed on the back of a pamphlet (for Baba Bhola B's Sex & VD Clinic), he said. "So, basically after you sum up the total from circle one and take the logarithmic root of this and add it to the square of the hyperbolic cosine of circle two- after subtracting that, of course- the dude with the higher number of points wins."

"You know Scooby, you could just fucking use the CAT Scores" Matar spoke up.

"Were you guys not listening?" Scooby asked, clearly agitated. "The Symbol S in Circle 2 refers to speed. So there are points for exiting the exam hall early. Symbol A_0 there" he said pointing to the relevant circle "is for accuracy. Symbol H_C here is for the number of hot chicks in your room. The DI sectional score's here..."

"Okay! Enough!" Matar yelled.

Bastard cleared his throat and gave Scooby a meaningful look. "Come on, tell them."

Scooby nodded. "If Bastard loses, he will ask out a guy and go out on three dates with him. At the end of the third date, he is to kiss the guy." There was a look of faraway sadistic pleasure on Scooby's face.

"And if you lose?" I queried.

"Go on Scoobo, tell them…" Bastard said, a quiet laugh playing at the corners of his mouth.

"I will not lose! I WILL NOT LOSE!" declared Scooby, his voice aquiver with emotion. He turned and rushed through the gates, leaving us baffled and Bastard laughing hysterically.

A week after CAT, a fortnight after Sem One exams and more than a month after summer placements, Delhi's winter was no longer an infant. It was surer of itself, its tantrums quite pronounced and debilitating.

I was in the CC, working on a presentation on my laptop when Matar showed up shivering.

"God, outside freezing!"

"What were you doing outside?" I asked.

"Fucking Media work" Matar said. "Some reporter had turned up and wanted to be shown around" he elucidated.

"Good yaar."

"What's good? It's fucking nothing- Media Relations. All we do is write media releases for everything that happens on campus, organize media coverage for the bloody conclaves- which isn't a difficult thing really- to be honest, the FMS name has a lot of bloody pull- and keep our website running." He took a breath and added, "And entertain reporters if they show up."

"That's quite enough, isn't it?" I asked.

"No it isn't. I mean our job should be something more. We should be out there keeping FMS in the news- not just keeping the news at FMS" he replied. "I would like us to do PR, BTL activities, student blogs, other shit- but saalee TMRGR keeps shooting everything I propose down."

TMRGR (short for T. M. R. Gopala Rau) was the senior who was Media Relations Secretary.

"Arre at least you guys are keeping busy man" I volleyed back. "There has been hardly any work at ConClub. First, our conclave got culled. Then the event we were thinking of organizing for Fiesta got buried as most of the sponsors & speakers pulled out. So, at our meeting this morning, all that was discussed was the specifics of the Return Party."

"Which fucking reminds me... because of your bloody 32K party, which beat our initiation party by quite a margin, TMRGR is insisting that the Return Party be at least a 40K thing just to be safe." He started toying with his turban in anger. "So that Media maintains its *legacy* of having the most expensive campus party."

An email announced itself on my laptop with a ping.

"What is it now? Another bloody GL?" asked Matar, still quite flustered.

"Nope... Some competition mail" I replied.

"You know HP, it's time we did a competition" Matar said, checking out his reflection in the glass of a nearby window "without making a royal public fool of ourselves."

I nodded my consent.

"There goes JENNA JAMESON!" Scooby announced loudly, emphasizing the name of the pornstar/ fictitious NBFC promoter.

Aastha (who looked as if she had heard) just walked away faster.

"Why so worked up, Scooby?" Matar posed.

"Damn woman. She's dieting you know" Scooby replied.

"So?" I asked.

"So, she asks for diet versions of everything. She wants diet Pepsi, diet popcorn, diet rice, diet soup. Then she says strawberry ice cream has more calories than vanilla and so we are condemned to eat vanilla..." Scooby paused to look back and scowl at Aastha, who stood at Anna's most likely ordering a diet samosa.

"Then she wants Sugar Free, which bhenchod costs ten times as much as sugar." Fumes arose from Scooby's nose, ears and mouth. "Next thing you know she's ordering some superexpensive foreign brand of water which according to her has fewer calories than Bisleri."

"Doc, does fucking water have calories?" Matar asked Bastard.

Bastard looked up from the Supercommando Dhruv comic he had been reading and said "Last time I studied medicine, it didn't."

"Guys! Deviation!" I interrupted. "The real question is how come you know all this, Scooby Dooby?"

Scooby looked away. "I just know..." he said quietly.

"Bata na saale" Matar too pleaded.

Scooby ignored him. He rubbed his hands together, blew air into them and muttered "Damn December! It's never been this cold", in a feeble attempt to change the topic.

"Scoooooobeeeeee" Bastard chanted.

Scooby sighed. "Fine, Doc!" He licked some sauce off our samosas' paper plate and began "I have been trying to get the group together again. I went out with them last week for a movie."

"Thursday. December 2nd", muttered Bastard, without looking up from his comic.

Scooby sighed.

"Wait! What group?" asked Matar and then understood as soon as he had spoken.

"The group we had. The Udupi waala group" Scooby replied looking slightly ashamed. "You know I was going to tell you guys."

There was a minute of silence before Matar said, "What's the fucking need, Scooby? Aren't we better off without those pricks?"

"Be that as it may" Scooby replied "unless you guys haven't noticed, the female to male ratio in our current group, sitting here eating samosas, is quite fucked up."

Bastard spoke up "He's been trying to get me to apologize to Ruchi for some time now." He yawned and resumed "But of course, that's not how he knows so much about Jenna Jameson's dieting plans."

"What the fuck, doc? Then tell me, how do I know?" Scooby shot back angrily.

Bastard waved off Scooby's volley and resumed reading the comic. Matar put a hand on Bastard's knee and said "Tell us, Basty."

"Elementary, my dear Matson" he said, sitting up from his relaxed perch on the plastic chair. "Note the anguish in Scooby's voice. It is the anguish of a man who has most likely singlehandedly funded the atrocious dieting plans of said mentally deficient female." His voice seemed different- possessed of a greater vivacity than usual. "As I have come to know Scoobson's character over our days together, I have understood him as a man who begrudges spending even a single rupee on anyone but himself. So my deduction is that Scoob here, went on a date."

"You fucking went on a date with Aastha?" Matar asked shocked.

Before Scooby could reply, Bastard stepped in. "Again, do not ignore the basics of logic, Matson. Said female is quite renowned for her mental deficiencies in the batch. Scoobster here, strikes me as a man who takes public opinion quite seriously. Also, were it a rendezvous with said deficient female, he wouldn't be sitting here, demeaning her publicly since that could- somewhere down the line- ruin the chances of him, how should I put it delicately, ah.... getting laid,."

"What the fuck, Bast..." Scooby began.

"Do not interrupt, kind sir!" Bastard resumed. "So we continue to traverse the path of logic and ask ourselves, who is the woman that our male subject has been enamored with, ever since we met?"

"Neelima" Matar & I said together.

"Correct! Further, the deficient female is the roommate of the love interest, i.e. Neelima. And based on my analysis of the mental deficiencies of aforementioned deficient female, I am prepared to believe that she tagged along with Neelima on what Scooby hoped was to be a romantic rendezvous. Thus, my diagnosis is that Scoob here went on a date with a Neelima, on which the dieting woman tagged along." His job done, Bastard leaned back into his relaxed bearing.

"Is this true, Scooby?" I asked.

Scooby was looking at Bastard angrily. "Yeah, it's true motherfucker" he said finally.

Matar patted Bastard. "Awesome, doc."

"Elementary" Bastard corrected him from behind the chronicles of Supercommando Dhruv.

The evening of that very day, Sem One results were declared. To our relief and slight disbelief, the four of us managed to pass in all the subjects that Semester One had subjected us to- even the Fin ones. Bastard topped amongst us with a top five rank. I was ranked a decent fifteenth in the batch with 65%. Matar was five marks below me while Scooby brought up the rear with an unflattering 56%. (FMS is among those rare B-schools in the country that does not indulge in comparative grading. However, the epidemic of competition sees students mention ranks on their CVs.)

As Delhi's winter became excruciating, we began to be subjected to lectures from companies, entrepreneurs, foreign university delegates and several other extras- most of which were organized for the purpose of attracting companies on campus for the upcoming lateral and then, final placements.

Let me take a minute and explain how the B-school industry works. Placements at a B-school are a delicate matter of maintaining a decent national rank over the years, getting the right corporates on campus at the right time, keeping the alumni happy (& drunk at alumni reunions), having foreign university tie-ups on your School's CV and of course other lesser factors as batch composition and the networking ability & will of the faculty. I might be missing a point here or there but this is largely it.

As laterals neared, the merry-go-round had come a full circle. The shadow of tension shifted to the seniors who could be seen preparing- mugging up things, reading texts or discussing funny sounding terms. There was an atmosphere of bottled jubilation and brimming confidence. The discussions of atrocious salaries and the multiplicity of companies (with big or big sounding names) descending on campus to give presentations had my mouth watering. I began to dream of a bungalow, of a chauffeur driven sedan, of expensive wrist watches and most of all, the happiness on Meenakhi's face when I could buy her anything she ever asked for.

As December progressed, Delhi's Winter had become as terrible and testy as Delhi itself. The Winter had an insatiable appetite. Noses ran, throats grew sore, ears grew red as anything and everything left uncovered by woolens, became his snack. It was very easy to be lazy- very difficult to wake up. The blanket was my piece of heaven- impossible to step out of.

And in this period of sleep and blankets, Matar & I started participating in marketing events, with our determination to crack an event (without the added corollary of making a fool of ourselves) counteracting our cold-induced laziness somewhat. The mechanics of the B-school events cog is usually such that the first stage involves presentations/ documents to be emailed to the respective B-school (organizing the event), on the basis of which people are shortlisted for the on-campus rounds. We kept shooting in the dark, emailing documents filled with jargon and bullcrap until we cracked it- the key to getting shortlists. Which was basically to make our presentation/ document as colorful/ vibrant/ beautiful as possible by filling it with graphs, figures, illustrations, etc.- all ploys to make it look like we were saying something intelligent when we actually weren't. Our first second round shortlist came from a marketing event at Fiesta (FMS' annual fest).

With a few days to go to our event, Matar & I were sitting in the library after classes, working on our ppt when a sullen Scooby and a visibly amused Bastard showed up.

"It's over" said Scooby gloomily.

"Oh yes, it's over" said Bastard, his tone dripping with mirth.

"What's over?" Matar asked. I pressed the Hibernate button and shut my laptop.

"Neelima" replied Scooby gloomy.

"Neelima" intoned Bastard humored.

"Well, her boyfriend's coming to town. So she said to me..." Scooby began.

Bastard cleared his throat. "Scoobson, tell the story from the beginning. The very beginning." He gave Scooby an encouraging pat and leaned back, eyes closed, his face contorted with impending bliss.

"Well, our first date was at McDonald's" Scooby began, a faraway dreamy look in his eyes.

"A date at McD? How fucking romantic!" Matar declared sarcastically.

"Anyway... we sat next to each other, her shoe touching mine. She complimented me on my shirt, then my hairstyle. I..."

"FUCKING DATE!" Matar exclaimed. "We were with you that day, remember?"

"Yeah, but you guys left before I did, didn't you?" Scooby retorted.

"So you spent what- five minutes of alone time with Neelima, Scooby?" I asked. "That was your date?"

"Twelve minutes. And yes, we flirted. She complimented me on my shirt. And my hairstyle."

Matar snorted. "Scooby, we compliment you on your fucking hairstyle sometimes. That's not quite flirting. And your chance meeting's not quite a date either."

"Do you not see, Matar?" Scooby began "Man- woman- flirting- food." He was counting these elements on his fingers. "That's a date!

End of story."

Bastard chortled. Sniggering myself, I proposed "Okay, let us assume that that thing was a date. What happened next?"

Scooby continued "Our second romantic excursion was a product of weeks of hard work and meticulous planning." Scooby replied in a tone that had forgotten the gloom of a few minutes ago. "Now I am only telling you guys this because we are the Kids; because we have secrets amongst us that we shall take to our graves." He held my eyes in a meaningful gaze. "Fellowmen, rejoice! For you are about to be introduced to the BanMad flowchart of love." He opened a book that lay in front of him to a blank page and began to explain.

"This here is the female" he explained, drawing what looked like an anorexic scarecrow. Two arrows emerged from the scarecrow. One said "Single" and the other said "Committed". Scooby set about drawing his flowchart with a fervent fury. Before we knew it, the whole page was covered in lines, arrows, circles, rhombuses and Scooby was explaining his fundas on how to get laid to a (largely) flabbergasted audience. Somewhere down the line, the arrows emerging from "Single" and those from "Committed" met again to flow to the final circle which was labeled "Sex".

Bastard seemed to have known of the BM Chart's existence beforehand and hence, looked quite the same. Or perhaps, he was just being his enigmatic self. Of the two of us, Matar recovered first. "You know, Scooby" he said pointing to the tenth circle on the Committed flow line "a fucking treat is not a date!"

Scooby held up four fingers. "Man. Woman. Food..."

I recovered at this point and cut him short. "So you ask them doubts, and do their assignments, and occupy their *mindspace* and...

and those other things in Circles three through seven… and um… what's that, say nasty things about their boyfriends before them. Scooby, isn't all this a bit too much?"

"No no no no no" Scooby replied, shaking his head dramatically. "A bit too much, my dear HP, is being single in a city like Delhi. A bit too much is every bloody decent woman in our class either having a boyfriend or being married or engaged. This is simply a scientific approach to getting a woman."

"But then it all went wrong at your second *date*, didn't it Scooby?" I questioned.

"I didn't count on that stupid female coming along" Scooby admitted. "Maybe I should make an addition to this flowchart somewhere." He looked at the BM Chart, lost in thought.

"You know Scooby" Matar spoke up "considering that your definition of a date is so fucking broad, I don't think Neelima even knew she was going on a date. Maybe she even asked Aastha to tag along."

"The surd has hit the nail on the head" Bastard announced. "Excellent, Matario! That is exactly the reason why what happened next, happened."

"Of course, she knew it *was* a date" Scooby reacted. Bastard waved his response off.

"So what happened next?" Matar asked.

"She met me today after the last lecture and made an unusual request" Scooby proceeded.

"Of a sexual nature?" Matar wondered.

"I wish" Scooby replied. "She requested me to drop her at this place at night. Where she was to meet her boyfriend."

"WHAT!" Matar & I exclaimed together. Bastard reacted by widening his grin.

Scooby continued "She really started pleading. She said she really needed my help… she said she… I was like… like her…" He seemed to be having trouble speaking.

Bastard cleared his throat and leaned forward. "She said she was like Scooby's behen."

All of us, except Scooby, burst out laughing.

"Wait, that's not all" Bastard said amid our peals of laughter. "Scoobhead ended up quite agitated by this. So he… he…" Bastard succumbed to laughter again.

"What next, Scooby?" Matar asked.

"Well, I reacted. It's one thing to reject a man's proposal. But to call him your brother…" Anger wrote itself on Scooby's face.

"What did you say then?" I inquired. Bastard had entered his thumping-things-around-him mode of laughter. I removed my laptop out of Bastard's zone.

"It came out. Almost instinctively. Without thought. I… I said…" One of Bastard's thumps dislodged the book with the recently etched BM Chart off the table.

Scooby heaved a sigh. "Well, I said- '*But I am a big behenchod.*'"

We dissolved to laughter. The table was vigorously thumped. Several books and concomitant pieces of stationery dislodged or hit in the crossfire. Several minutes later, after the hilarity died, after we had blown our noses and cleared our eyes of laughter water, we discovered Scooby sitting gloomily, tinkering with his flowchart.

Fiesta's event passed without bestowing a reward upon Matar &

me. But I felt content to have made it to the final five from among fifty odd entries nationally. We sat & learnt (from our competitors) the most important/ only thing that a B-school can teach you- the art of making a presentation.

As Semester Two's inhabitants- freer than ever before, now that the only thing consuming us was academics or GLs where we had hardly any incentive to actually listen, time passed in a flurry. It was perhaps a month or two of freedom and though it was perhaps the happiest period of my MBA, all my memories of this period are of my own story.

My characters, the sons of God and sons of Devil that made up my story were keeping me in a fugue. I was writing them into existence more & more each day- their apparition grew stronger with every word I wrote and their existence stronger with each apparition. I was a rat in a cage walking the wheel of my story, totally consumed and concussed. I am sure Matar must have thought I was going insane.

The many sons of Gods & sons of Devils of the senior batch had a divine placement season. Laterals and finals both ended in a matter of days with people actually being spoilt for choice. Several people (Mowgli included) had a happy confusion between multiple job offers. (Mowgli had three placement offers- two PPO's he had- one from his summers firm and the other from a competition he had won and a final job offer during laterals.) Average salary saw a 30% jump over the previous year and most importantly, even the lowest salary on campus- the figure Matar & I pegged our future hopes to, was significantly higher than the salaries we had left to come to FMS and than what we thought we deserved.

Battle, Field

You put a hundred insects in a box- lock them up and they'll find a way to co-operate, to coexist. You put a hundred of the arguably most brilliant minds in the country in a room- lock them up and most will not leave alive.

As Year One came to a close and as we went from MSA review (where ConClub was incidentally lynched for doing nothing all year) to the structure GBM (where the societies' structure for the subsequent year was argued, disagreed, squabbled & finally decided upon) to society elections, the class had become a warzone. We were no longer one batch but a summation of camps, prominent among them a hostellers' gang, a Delhiites gang, an 8 by 8 gang and the Khullas. It was Game Theory in practice; we were all entrapped in what Strategy calls Prisoner's Dilemma. Unsure of how much the other prisoner would confess, you ended up confessing to everything at your end, thereby condemning both your accomplice and yourself. In simpler terms, you set fire to everything around you, thinking that if I am burning, at least let everybody burn.

By the time it all ended, by the time society structures had been decided and PlaceCom & Presidents elected to posts, we were wet logs with sparks simmering underneath- a fire that would take months to die down and a moment to reignite.

I must say good sense prevailed in the end- the right men were elected to the right posts (for the most part). But the sheer hideous nakedness of humankind revealed, pissed me off. In fact, Scooby was the only one amongst the four of us who decided to continue as a society member, even after the bloodletting and the etching of boundaries & No Man's lands between camps, akin to those between nation states.

I found Bastard at Anna's, iPod in ear- twirling two pens violently, beating a set of imaginary drums. He opened his eyes to hit the snare and found me staring at him curiously, like everybody else at Anna's.

"RHCP... Awesome drummer" he explained.

I smiled and sat down across him. Bastard took the earphones out of his ears and relieved the pens of their twirling responsibilities. We sat in silence, two friends enjoying the gentle warmth of each other's company in the cold of Delhi's winter & MBA's wars.

"Mat & Scoob?" he asked after some time.

"Have gone to get some notes photocopied" I replied.

Bastard nestled in to his chair further and sighed. "So what's bothering you, Hariman?"

"Is it that obvious?" I asked.

Bastard grinned & nodded.

"Well, she's leaving. For US. Says it's some family reason. It just... just hurts to know she's farther away." I found my voice choking slightly.

"How long?"

"Six months she says. She's... she's left with her mother & sister." I felt a tear or two building up in my eyes.

Bastard closed his eyes and pushed his head back a little. When he spoke his voice was soft, almost a whisper. "Hari, if your love is strong & true, it will persevere. No matter how far away Meenakshi is."

For some stupid reason, I felt better. There is something to a reassurance, a friend saying that it will turn out alright, that makes your fears go away- makes your dream believable. I sat in the winter chill, warmed by Bastard's faith in my love.

But there was more to the chill than just Delhi's tantrums or love's woes. Anna's, which used to be a buzz of chit- chat & frolic, was the World Map as the battles had etched it. The eight or so round tables around which the plastic chairs were set up, (to continue indulging in my World War analogy) belonged to the various camps- the Germans, the Japs, the Anglo- Saxons, etc., one table comprising me & Bastard- at best, a refugee camp; and the last table comprised of the non aligned- people brought together by the singular fact that they did not belong to any other camp.

I do not know how but Bastard noted that I noted.

"Don't worry. This too shall pass" he said.

"Or get worse" I retorted.

"Either way, this zoo is a good lesson for our impending corporate slavery" Bastard stated. "We'll meet worse animals in the jungle out there."

For the umpteenth time, I wondered why I had voluntarily consented to be a part of the zoo.

Our study circle convened a day before the first exam of Sem Two.

"So her boyfriend's still here? In Delhi?" Matar asked.

"Yes, Matar. He is still here" Scooby replied quietly.

Five minutes of momentous mugging later, the conversation resumed. "So, what does Neelima's BF do?" I asked.

"I-Banker" Scooby replied grumpily. "Earns more in a month than I did in six."

Matar indulged himself to a villainous mocking laugh. "Sorry, Scooby. Guess you got fucked."

Scooby mumbled something incoherent and began to underline his notes furiously.

"Hey, what about your CAT bet? Wasn't the fucking CAT result a month or two ago?" Matar wondered.

Scooby looked up from the photocopied notes he was mugging up, to nod. Bastard looked up from his laptop screen to stare at Scooby.

Scooby succumbed to Bastard's gaze a minute later. He began "Well we agreed…" Bastard cleared his throat. "Okay okay… I begged Doc to put off the bet until the society bullshit and exams ended."

"Who won?" I asked.

Bastard raised his middle finger languidly. Scooby nodded disconsolately.

"So when is Scooby doing whatever he is doing?" Matar asked, his voice brimming with humor.

"After exams, Matarfucker! Let me study now!" Scooby exclaimed, agitated.

Bastard laughed.

"Bata na Basty. What is it?" Matar appealed.

"It's nothing!" Scooby replied angrily. "Now let me study or I'll be the first person in the history of FMS to fail Mark-Research."

The last day of Sem Two exams, Scooby was dressed in the unbeatable combo of a dark strawberry colored shirt and light pink leather jeans. Matar remarked how the tight jeans accentuated Scooby's small bony buttocks and it was then quite impossible to get the revolting image out of my head. More than once I found myself involuntarily writing 'buttocks' in my answer sheet, which I then had to carefully strike out.

For the first time, Bastard did not leave the exam hall well in advance of the three hours allotted. After (apparently) finishing his paper, he sat staring intently at Scooby seated ahead of us, occasionally twirling pens playing non- existent percussion.

I finished the paper five minutes before end of time and gave my paper a cursory revision. Bastard was seated with arms folded now, clearly in anticipation of something. Matar & Scooby were still writing.

As the bell for the end of time tolled and the invigilators collected the papers, Bastard stood up, arms still folded, staring at Scooby. Scooby took a lot of time in collecting his stationery, admit card and question paper- one thing or the other seemed to keep falling off. "It happens now" said a whisper. I found Matar by my side, his beard hairs slightly askew from examination blues.

"The bet?" I asked.

"Hell yeah."

Scooby seemed to have finally mustered his belongings and his courage. He turned to give Bastard a last-ditch pleading look, which was waved off and dismissed.

"Not in front of everyone!" Scooby beseeched.

"The time is NOW" replied the bet winner.

And then, just as Neelima was passing him, Scooby said "Wait!"

Neelima and Anu (one of her babe- friends) waited.

Scooby sighed. "I have something to say to you."

"Me?" asked Neelima.

Scooby uttered a small 'Yes'. He then turned his back to Neelima so that the aforementioned small bony rear- end cushions faced her (& us).

It began with a slight wobble of the small bony contraptions which eventually graduated to a committed gyration. And when this disgusting yet strangely hypnotic vibration of Scooby's ass was at its maximum attainable/ terminal velocity, Scooby howled "Oooooooo! Scooooby Doooooby Doooooooo!"

Neelima was the first to burst out laughing. Scooby continued for a minute or two, until everyone had noticed (and yielded to laughter) - even the invigilator who was counting the papers. And after the gyration cum howling was discontinued, after Neelima had rushed out of the hall laughing maniacally- amid the enduring peals of laughter, the entire class- all of her camps- howled "Ooooooooooooo! Scooooooooby Dooooooooby Dooooooooooo!" as one.

Summerzzz

End of Year One meant the beginning of summer internships. Matar & Bastard proceeded to Mumbai to serve their multinational giant hirers; Scooby was shipped to Chennai to help a certain bank sell more of its credit cards.

Matar told me he would be wearing a suit. Scooby's email said that there was no way he would be wearing a suit in Chennai's heat (he claimed he would be wearing his "bicep flaunting" black Tee and shorts). Bastard was non- committal.

I decided to take Matar's advice and wear a business suit on April 6th, my first day at Blue Zone. It was perhaps due to this fact that I was called "Sir" and saluted by the guard at the gate, the liftman and finally wished "Good Morning Sir" quite respectfully to, by several employees at the office.

The Blue Zone office was located on the seventh floor of Crystal Towers in Gurgaon. It was located between the offices of Tuborg and Foster's. The receptionist looked appropriately red eyed and hung over. She took my visiting card and asked me ("*Sir*") to sit and wait.

As I sat on the extremely comfortable sofa that felt like a holiday for the buttocks, I was served tea and was apologized quite profusely to for the fact that my point of contact in the company was busy in a meeting. I accepted the apologies, waved them off, gorged on a premium brand of biscuits and tea, flipped through a business magazine from the stack the receptionist had laid out for me ("*Sir*").

The Air Conditioner was caressing my face comfortably, the tea & biscuits made me feel satiated, my buttocks were still on holiday in Sofa World; I fell asleep with my mouth open in what was quite an unprofessional manner. When I came to, I found a young guy calling "Hari? Hari Parmeshwar?"

I sat up. "Rough night, eh?" I looked up. He was not quite as young as my first impression of him had been. His clothes were sharp and formal, his watch flashy & expensive, his expression relaxed & slightly humored. "Hi. I am Rohit. We have interacted on email."

Rohit Gupta- I recalled. My appointed mentor for the internship. I stood up abruptly and shook his extended hand. "Come on. Follow me" he said. And as we were passing the receptionist, he said to her in mock exasperation "He's the intern, Sheila."

Sheila said "Oh" and I knew I would not be called "Sir" or served tea & expensive biscuits again.

Rohit took me through a maze of rooms, offices, etc. before he found what he was looking for. He ushered me into a Sem Hall sized room- an empty conference hall by the looks of it and told me that he would be busy in meetings through the day. He asked me to meet him at 6 in the evening, handed me a few files he wanted me to go through and left.

The room was made of glass walls on all sides. I noticed that the entire office was glass walls- some of them obscured by a whitish coloring for the bottom half with the Blue Zone logo on top. I settled into a chair which wasn't nearly as much fun as the sofa that loved buttocks.

The files were quite boring. Apparently, Blue Zone was a technology consulting firm that handled software projects for other firms. The files were filled with technical details of projects, one of them was purely dedicated to Blue Zone's history. Needless to say, I was quite bored- the only things keeping me awake were the absence of the sofa- soft and the grammatical or spelling errors in the project reports.

I was laughing at "... the comapny is intends to growl at 20% per annum..." when I heard a knock on the door and a rotund male face made itself visible.

"Hari?" Rotund male face asked.

I nodded.

"Come with me."

Rotund Male Face was called Mohan Shetty. I was pleasantly surprised to know that he came from the same engineering college as me. He was in fact, two years my junior. We talked of college, some of the assholic profs, some of the good ones and then the female hotties. (Everybody remembers hot females in an engineering campus. Forever.)

"Remember Nidhi Vashisht, Haribhai?" he asked, smacking his lips.

Of course I remembered Nidhi Vashisht. We had been in the same Chemistry Lab group once; only the acrid chemicals had kept me from falling in love.

"She's on Zee Tv now... in some serial" Shetty added.

"Wow."

"And Megha Jhalla? Remember her?" Shetty posed.

As we conversed, Shetty led me to the cafeteria where he got us coffee from a dispenser. Over coffee, we recalled & discussed hot females one by one, until we were bored. Though you'll still find people play this game everywhere, there's not much to discus once a hottie's name has been mentioned except vital stats or meaningless incidents like "I picked up a book she dropped once; she smiled at me" or "She once shared a seat on a bus with me."

We then talked about what Blue Zone did (aside from growling at 20% per annum). And then what he did at Blue Zone. Shetty appeared to be happy and content with his job. He told me that he wanted to stay a techie, that he was super-happy at Blue Zone and that he was never going to do an MBA.

We chatted for an hour or so until Shetty realized that a meeting he was supposed to be in, had started thirty minutes ago. He left me to my coffee and my devices, advising me to meet Maheshwari who would help me with my employee ID and related things.

I found Maheshwari after twenty odd minutes of playing the maze. Maheshwari was a middle aged babu who seemed more interested in his tea (which he sipped at a deathly slow rate) than anything else in the world. His preoccupation with the beverage meant that he took half an hour to enter me into the employee database. It took him twenty odd very small sips more to issue me an employee ID card.

On my way back, I got lost again. I entered a room of someone (who looked quite old, well paid and senior management) by mistake, apologized, got out, asked a peon for directions, took a wrong turn from the vending machine and fifteen minutes later, returned to the spot I had started from. The peon took pity on me and walked me to my room.

At 5:59 PM, I appeared at Rohit's door, tie straightened, suit buttoned and hair pasted in place by water. I saw him on the phone through the glass walls of his cage, simultaneously typing something on his laptop. I knocked with an increasing degree of force until he heard and looked up. He motioned for me to come in and sit.

I entered and sat quietly, letting Rohit do whatever he was doing. There was a picture of him and a good looking woman on his table, who I assumed was his wife. Other than that, his table was devoid of any personal effects. The wall behind him (which being the same as the outer wall of the office premises) was made of concrete (and not glass) and was covered by framed certificates, all of whom appeared to have been awarded for attending some sort of Blue Zone Workshops. I marveled at the amount of phony CV points he had accumulated, ranging from "Workshop on Team Building" to "Workshop on Family & Time Management."

Some ten minutes later the telephonic conversation ended, although the typing on the laptop continued. There was a Blue Zone logo on the inclined stand on which the laptop rested and under it was emblazoned "Ergonomic Holder." Rohit took a break from the typing, cricked his neck and cracked his knuckles (in a manner that was hardly ergonomic) and looked at me studiously. "So Mr. Parmeshwar, read those files?"

I had read them quite diligently. Taken notes. "Yes sir" I replied confidently.

"Good" he said. Then abruptly, he turned the ergonomic holder, so that I could see his laptop's screen. "So, let me explain to you a few things that would come handy in your project."

And that was the last word I understood. From then on until the meeting ended, I was in a first year FinSoc session again, nodding politely without understanding a word. I have no clue what he was explaining or attempting to accomplish by explaining- not the slightest idea whether it was finance or technology or marketing or gobbledygook.

He spoke for forty five minutes or so, showing me all sorts of files on his laptop- ppts with garish animations (one of the slides on "Process Flow" had a flowing river pasted on top), lengthy word files or Excels with vast oceans of numbers, all of whose magics and mysteries I was supposed to grasp in the cursory seconds long glances Rohit allowed me.

At the end, for some reason, he gave me a pen and paper and asked me to do a calculation ("Try and find out the DTRI Percentage"). Totally zapped, I wrote a lot of random numbers on the paper, connected a few with arrows, circled others and eventually, toe fingers crossed replied "42?"

"Close enough" Rohit said and smiled, clearly pleased. He then embarked on another round of drivel, taking me through bewildering statements like "...the impact of ARR on DTRI numbers, when capitalized..." I switched my brain off and relaxed my posture, hoping I would not have to make another random calculation again.

I was let off at quarter past seven and advised to "*keep these things in mind*" while doing my internship.

Since that meeting on my first day, Rohit didn't find the time to meet me. Often, he would ask me to wait till late in the evening and then, promptly forget about me & head home. Or he would ask me to meet him the following day and then reschedule. Eventually, I gave up and decided to loiter around & fritter away my time, watching '*How I Met Your Mother*' on my laptop or indulging in binges of free coffee in the cafeteria. It wasn't a matter of running away from work; there simply was none.

Shetty helped me get a workstation- basically some desk space, an internet connection and a creaky chair. I sat amid people doing "all kinds of things", shamelessly watching the exploits of Ted Mosby or chatting online with Scooby, Matar or Bastard or thinking about Meenakshi.

Another week passed before I got to know the title of my project. On my eleventh working day, on Shetty's prodding & probing, someone in the HR department sent me an email which stated that I had to set some sort of metrics in place for measuring past and future project profitablities. I made a note of the project title in my notebook and graduated to Season Three of HIMYM.

Day fifteen, Rohit finally found time for me again and asked me about the progress I had made on my project. I still don't know why he thought I had made any progress at all. I mumbled something on the lines of "...making good progress..." which he accepted as a reply for some reason.

He began to drivel again. This time, however, I understood the odd word or phrase here and there but brought together none of it still made any sense at all. After a point, he started repeating some of the same nonsense he had discoursed in our first meeting. Excels, documents, PDFs, ppts were shown. We visited the flowing river again.

"So Mr. Parmeshwar" he said. "Understood everything, right?"

I nodded hesitantly.

"Good. So for your mid review, make a presentation on these

issues and how you propose we resolve them."

I nearly fell off my chair. Rohit didn't notice the look of shock on my face and continued driveling.

Half an hour later, he let me go saying he had some important meeting to go to. Extricating myself from Rohit's Chamber of Mysteries & Riddles, I set about in search of Shetty who I hoped would help me decode somewhat what Rohit wanted me to do.

"A double MBA?"

Shetty nodded.

"But why? Why? Why? Why? Why? Who... Who does MBA twice?"

Shetty replied mid- gorge allowing me a rather unpleasant view of semi- digested burger components. "Loads of people do. Especially if the first MBA is from a so-so institute."

"But isn't Rohit from IIML? That's not a so-so institute, right?" I wondered.

Shetty thankfully swallowed before answering this time. "That's his second MBA. His first one was from Amity or IIPM or IGIT or someplace like that."

"IGIT has an MBA programme?" This was a morning of revelations.

Shetty laughed at the look on my face. "Haribhai, my point is MBA's are mad. And when you do two MBA's, you become doubly mad. That's Rohit Gupta to you. There are two people this office employs just to decode what he says. But he has his advantages."

"Advantages?"

"Yeah. Like if we have to make a pitch to a prospective client, we let him speak for a few minutes. Or let him take the questions." He let off a loud burp. "The clients, of course, do not understand a word he says. But they usually think he is saying something high-end consult- types… something that only our company knows… and sign us in a hurry."

"Wow."

"Yup" Shetty concluded.

A tubelight in the corner flickered on after several minutes of struggle. Something clicked in my head. "So, does it also work the other way round? I mean does Rohit understand completely what people are saying to him?"

Shetty chewed over my question a minute before answering. "Never thought of it that way before. Come to think of it, Haribhai, I don't think anybody's ever taken him seriously enough to care." He whipped up a fragment of lettuce leaf that had contrived to stay out of his bites. "Don't worry about him. He'll most likely forget about this mid review thing."

He did. But not the way I would have liked him to. When I ran into Rohit a day or two later, I found that he had somehow managed to get hold of the thought that he had asked me to do some kind of a survey, surveying only God knows what. He rambled on about things that had begun to sound familiar now, without making sense.

Piecing together the forensic evidence, Shetty and Rishabh (one of Rohit's henchmen) deciphered that he (most likely) wanted me to do a client survey for Blue Zone. For which I would need to contact clients. For which I would need security clearances from Head Office that were likely to take weeks. They advised me to forget all about it and avoid Rohit like the plague.

And so I did. But just to be on the safe side, I devoted my time to applying for clearances (that never came) and cc'ed all of my numerous mails to Rohit. When no response came, I had worked towards having one of the most important advantages in Corporate India on my side. Plausible Deniability.

The first paycheque did it. Nearly a month into the internship, it found its way to me through Blue Zone's intricate system of intra office communication. As I opened the envelope and a green tinged cheque fell out promising me a sum slightly higher than my last salary at ABC, I felt exhilaration thump through my veins. I felt like a businessman. I felt wealthy and important.

But the feeling quickly withdrew, leaving in its wake painful dregs of guilt. However much I justified my non-performance on Rohit's insanity or the lack of any seriousness about my internship at Blue Zone, point was that I had just been paid for doing absolutely nothing. And somewhere this hurt.

So I started. With very little help from Rohit, I set about dropping in on people or meeting them through Shetty, trying to make some sense about how the wheels at Blue Zone turned and more importantly about what the scope of my project was- what I was supposed to do. It took more than a week to figure everything out- my deliverables (which I emailed to Rohit, without him replying back), how & where I could get the data I needed from and what I would do with it.

It took twenty odd trips to the basement (where the Blue Zone Data Centre was), befriending people, pleading, begging, scratching some backs to lay my hands on the numbers I wanted. Once I had the hundreds of Excel files filled with project financials, it took me even more time to figure out what to do with them. In the last two weeks of my internship, I visited and revisited aspects of finance that had either been forgotten after summers or had originally been too big sounding for me to hitherto even attempt to understand. And then, I had to contend with the fact that the financial data was in a non uniform format across files which made running Macros- Microsoft Excel's divine gift of automation- across them impossible.

Hence I did it all manually. The real world equivalent of which is manually constructing the Empire State Building, brick by brick, in two weeks.

The very last day of my internship, after days of pestering, Rohit finally got around to booking one of the conference rooms to let me present the fruits of my labor. The presentation was attended by Rohit, Shetty, Rishabh and the old senior management guy (who I found was called Bhatia) whose room I had wandered into on the first day.

The presentation went quite well. Though I started off nervous, I grew in confidence as I progressed and nobody challenged the veracity of my findings or methods. Rohit interrupted frequently but only to (apparently) support my findings with directionless drivel. Bhatia, on the other hand, sat quietly watching me intently and interrupted only once or twice- that too with factual queries. By the time I reached the last slide an hour or so later, I had grown in confidence enough to loosen my tie, roll up my sleeves and talk to them as if I was an experienced expert on finance and not the first year MBA passout whose knowledge of finance was limited to a Madhu Vij book and Google.

I finished with a flourish, summing up my suggestions confidently. Bhatia asked me a few questions which I managed to answer to his satisfaction. Rohit said some things- everyone in the room politely nodded to- without understanding fully. We closed to light applause.

As I rolled down my sleeves & pulled up my tie, wondering what had gotten into me and as everyone started to get up to leave, Bhatia came up to me. He shook my hand with a flourish and said "Good job, Hari. Your suggestions will help us a great deal." I felt more wealthy, important and businessman-like than I'd ever had all my life.

Recess Ion

Though he was the same, Matar looked different somehow. I stared at him awkwardly for a few seconds trying to put a finger on what had changed in him. He took my hand-extended for a shake and pulled me into a hug.

"Hari, my boy" he said, slapping my back, "Fucking nice to see you again. *MDI ka hostel kaisa tha*?" (I had stayed in the MDI hostel during summers.)

I mumbled something and continued to stare at him. It was his beard, I thought. It looked different somehow. But as we began to talk, swapping tales of our internships, I realized that it too was the same. Perhaps I had simply forgotten what Matar looked like.

"…and then he says '*Dal gayee CD?*' I could not help but laugh. Here I am presenting what is probably the fucking presentation of my life and this guy- a VP by the way- is talking to his wife explaining how to… You listening Hari?"

I wasn't really but I nodded. Matar went on. The story of his presentation continued until his phone beeped.

"Message from Bastard. Report to college" he announced.

"What?"

"That's all it says. Report to college."

We descended from our PG into Kamla Nagar's overcrowded markets and started walking. There was a difference in the market too. Several shops had changed the color on their signages. Some of them had simply shut down or been replaced. But it was quite barely visible. Delhi's change. Even though Delhi looked infinitesimally different from when I had left it, it was still the same.

It took us twenty minutes to walk to college. By then, Matar's summers story had progressed to the point where he had been denied a PPO[1] . We were about to embark on the story of Matar's unreceived stipend cheque, when we found Scooby and Bastard talking in low voices at Anna's.

"What the fuck is '*Report to college*'?" Matar asked angrily.

"Shhh..." Scooby raised a finger to his lips.

"Don't you shush me, Scooby. And what's that fucking atrocity of a growth you have on your face?" Matar yelled loudly.

"I believe it's a French beard, Mathead" Bastard replied. "But I have my reservations too."

"Get up assholes. Is this the way to greet your bros?" Matar said in mock exasperation.

Matar gave both Bastard and Scooby hugs. I hugged Scooby and shook hands with Bastard.

We sat down.

---

[1]Pre Placement Offer

"Why have we *reported* to college?" Matar asked in the general direction of Bastard & Scooby. "Session doesn't start till Monday."

Scooby suddenly got up and rushed towards Anna's counter. There was one other person standing there, waiting most likely for Anna to return his change or convert his money into food.

"What's up with him?" I asked.

"You'll see" Bastard replied mysteriously.

I almost missed it. Everything happened so fast that my mind just about processed it.

"Bastard, did I just see Scooby punch Raman? And run away?" I asked bewildered. I looked sideways at Matar who was staring at Raman openmouthed.

"Well, yes" Bastard said. Raman was on his haunches now, breathing heavily. Anna stared at him bemused.

"What the fuck, Doc? What just happened?" Matar asked.

"Scooby's been drinking" Bastard replied. He patted his chest pocket where I knew the vodka flask rested.

"So he's punching people?" I wondered.

"Not people, Hariman, no. Just Raman" Bastard said. He stretched his arms and looked at us cheerfully.

"Bastard!" Matar exclaimed.

Bastard laughed. "Well to tell the story anticlimactically, Raman is Neelima's new… no, newest boyfriend."

Matar swore something funny. Raman spat something that looked like blood from distance.

"Raman? When? How?" I sputtered.

"Ah, the 'When' takes me back to Ben Bernanke. As for the 'How'…"

Matar cut him short. "Bastard, fucking stop talking in fucking riddles. Stop being fucking... fucking Bastard."

"Fair point" Bastard retorted. He took out his flask and took a swig. "Okay, here's the dope. One- Sub prime crisis. Two- recession. Three, Baam! I-banker loses his job. Four" Bastard paused to take another swig "Neelima decides- without job, I-banker not so lovable. Five, walks in Raman with rich dad and big car. Six, Scooby punches Raman." Bastard took a lazy bow.

"Wow" Matar said softly.

"Wow indeed" Bastard replied.

"But... but... it can't be. Maybe she left him for some other reason, Bastard" I reasoned. "Maybe, maybe she..."

"Let's do the math, HP" he replied. "Why would she then choose the wealthiest guy on campus? And not the guy who everybody knows has been smitten with her, ever since he laid eyes on her?"

"Fucking gold-digger" Matar muttered.

"Welcome to the recession, my angels" Bastard said cheerily. "When the rich find love. When Scooby gets screwed."

"I never thought Neelima could..." Matar let the sentence hang.

"The malaise is spreading fast, boys" Bastard said. "Neelima. Vinita. Shilpa" he counted the names on his fingers as he spoke. "And Ruchi. Aastha though is still clinging to hers."

"Wait, Ruchi?" I asked, baffled. "Wasn't she single?"

"Oh no, HP. That's what she liked us all to believe" Bastard replied. "Ruchi's just switched her boyfriend from MDI to IIM. And if word on street's to be believed, she traveled all the way to Indore to *seal the deal.*"

After a few minutes of silence Matar spoke up "That said, Doc, did you incite Scooby?"

Bastard shrugged. "I like to believe the world is a bit fairer now" he replied without answering.

The commencement of Second Year meant the entry of a fresh batch of bright eyed fuchhas. The few women amongst them were surveyed, indexed, rated, added as friends on Orkut/ Facebook and fought over. Praxis, the society in charge of issuing mentees to famished male seniors, was issued claims ("She's from my college, na..."), pleas ("I'll do all your assignments..."), prayers and death threats.

Some incredible compromise had come to pass between Raman & Scooby (presided over by Bastard) and the matter was never spoken of again. Scooby recovered from the heartbreak with his French beard and three female mentees he assigned himself (blatantly abusing his post as a senior member of Praxis).

I remember myself being in a constant state of agitation in this period. Though I was quite unaware of the causes at that point, I believe it was a combination of several factors. My faith in love was being shattered bit by bit everyday. And there were horror stories of recession coming in everyday. Several of my friends employed at ABC or otherwise were being laid off. The dream of the expensive watch, chauffeur driven sedan and my happy fish eyed love seemed to be getting hazier by the day.

I decided to take MBA, life, everything seriously. This was not the time for frolic, staying off academics till exams or indulging myself to my fancies of writing- I felt. I was Hari Parmeshwar, worried MBA student of Recession's Wars, straightening my tie in the mirror of my mind. I pushed my story & my writer into a shoebox.

I looked over my CV and found that it was my skills at MS Word (to a large extent) that had enabled me to fill one A4 sized page with gas. If I had to get myself to fill two pages for Finals with stuff, I had to get cracking at two things (which are usually among the ten most used words at FMS every year, without fail)- Events & Live Projects.

So while registering, applying and sending entries for almost every marketing event that I came across, I started preparing and presenting, often singlehandedly, almost every single presentation that we were obligated to give in class. In a few weeks, as people belonging to my groups had come to assume I would be doing everything everyweek & begun to free ride, I found myself growing in confidence and my gyaan, communication & presentation skills increasing exponentially. By the time we were two months into the second year, I had started to win marketing events and people had begun referring to me as a 'Marketing God.'

The Live Projects proved infinitely harder to crack. A whole lot of swindlery happens at almost every campus across the country- with regards to shortlists for campus representations at competitions, industry projects and even placements but I found myself growing in anger & frustration as despite having built one of the stronger marketing CVs on campus, I got no shortlists at all. But I took it in my stride; took my search for industry projects offline.

Eventually, Matar, Scooby & I got a live project in healthcare marketing, through one of Bastard's contacts. It wasn't much work really but as it came to fill white space on our CV's, it looked & sounded good.

To celebrate one of Matar and my biggest ticket ever wins in a national event, the clique convened at our PG with booze and chips (sponsored by yours truly). Delhi's August sun stared at me from the screen of Scooby's laptop. After a few minutes of procrastination, I finally decided to get up to pull the blinds and the reflection died.

"Scoobster, you can stop pointing now. We get the point" Bastard grumbled.

"No you don't. I want you guys to fully appreciate the magnitude of the situation. She is bigger and better than last season. Wait... Wait..." Scooby held up his index finger. "Extent of the situation. Ah, better..." he continued, snapping his fingers "Enormity of the situation."

"Scooby, can we watch just one episode of HIMYM without objectifying women?" I asked. Matar snored louder as if in agreement.

Scooby thought it over a few seconds before saying "No, Hari, I don't think we can. The situation" his pointing finger returned to the screen "is too *massive* to not do so. In fact, Hari..."

"Shut up, Scoobster."

Scooby shut up but continued to point.

I sighed and turned my attention to the Economic Times editorial I had been intending to read for a long time. Some economist was talking about what some were calling the worst recession since 1929 and its impact on India.

"Fucking decoupling" I muttered.

Both Scooby and Bastard turned and stared at me.

"What?" I asked.

"Stay off Matar for a few days, HP" Bastard suggested, laughing.

"Anyway why is decoupling to be fucked?" Scooby chipped in. "It is a perfectly good sounding word. Decoupling. Deeeeee..."

I threw my pillow at Scooby. He ducked and it missed & hit the cracked mirror instead.

"It's such a stupid theory" I said. "There is no way we could have been insulated from this mess."

"Maybe" said Bastard. "And maybe not."

"Hey, I have one!" Scooby exclaimed. "Dee. Cup. Ling. You see where I am going with that." Scooby's hands were committed to an inappropriate posture. "D... Cup..."

I threw my Nokia at Scooby. He caught it and continued to chant "D- Cup- Ling".

"Where's the violence coming from, Hari?" Bastard inquired.

"Why maybe not?" I asked, somewhat angrily.

Bastard sighed and smiled sagaciously. "Economies are elephants, Hariman. Any event... every event is like a whisper in their ear... telling them to change course. Shut up, Scooby!" Scooby toned down the volume on the "D- Cup" song.

Bastard continued. "Of course, said global meltdown is more than a whisper. More like a bang. But, Hariman, we never know how the elephants will react. We can make some very good guesses, yes, but we can never be sure."

"My feeling is we are all going down, Bastard" I replied morosely. "The world is coming to an end."

"Depression in a recession?" Scooby exclaimed. "HP! Recession is nothing but... but a... a..."

"Fact of life for the elephants" Bastard concluded.

"No! It's just an ion, my engineer friend." Scooby proclaimed merrily. "A recess ion! It will find its oppositely charged mate and die."

I threw a pen at Scooby. It missed.

"I still think the world is coming to an end" I said heatedly.

Scooby laughed.

On September 15 [illegible] by an act of financial terrorism, Lehman died. Bear Stearns, Citi, Merrill Lynch, J. P. Morgan, Morgan Stanley and every big sounding financial name I had heard of were all admitted [illegible]

Lehman

And then the world began to end.

Half a globe away, some incredibly smart people- no doubt MBA's- had been caught with their pants down, undergarments missing and genitals mauled. To put it mildly.

On September 15th by an act of financial terrorism, Lehman died. Bear Sterns, Citi, Merril Lynch, J. P. Morgan, Morgan Stanley- and every big sounding financial name I had heard of- were all admitted to Intensive Care. The dream jobs, the high paying recruiters at FMS (& campuses across the country) were now either dead or comatose or badly disfigured at the very least.

But dear reader, you are yet to fully understand or appreciate the stupidity of the creature called the MBA student. Buoyed by the fact that the first years' summer placements were relatively decent (considering the meltdown), this creature turned down Pre Placement Offers across the country- assuming that the downtrend worth hundreds of billions of dollars in toxic assets was either limited to impacting the US or to impacting tier two B-schools.

A total of 22 PPO's were offered at FMS. 12 were accepted.

The Sky spewed torrents of rain in anger. Maybe it too had invested in a CDO[1] that was now worth less than the puddle of water beside Matar's foot.

"So are you accepting?" Scooby asked.

This was supposed to be Bastard's PPO party. As a mark of respect to the state of the world, it was a relatively austere bash at DSE tea stall.

Bastard appeared to have not heard. He continued to look dreamily into the distance, taking occasional sips of his spiked tea. And then, when we had all looked away, he spoke softly. "Of course I am."

A cloud thundered angrily in the distance. "But that's not important" he continued. "Has she called yet?" he asked, looking at me.

I caressed the Nokia in my pocket wishing it were her hand and shook my head.

"Has who called yet?" Scooby asked.

"She's back?" Matar asked.

"Who's back?" Scooby asked.

"Meenakshi" I whispered.

A moment of silence ensued. A stray dog, drenched in recession's rains, came up to us and stared at us with hopeful eyes.

"When was the last time you talked to her, HP?" Scooby inquired.

[1]Collaterized Debt Obligation- one of the primary causes of the Subprime Crisis

"Her last email was a few weeks ago, maybe" I replied.

"No, HP. Talk, as in... talk to her. Using your voice" Scooby said.

"I don't know, Scooby" I said. "Don't really remember."

"So let me get this straight. Your *girlfriend* and you haven't talked in months?" Scooby queried, starting to get a little worked up.

"We are different, Scooby" I replied.

"GODDAMN!" Scooby exploded. "Let me tell you this, Hari. Let me make it plain and... and... and..."

"Simple" Bastard offered.

"Yes, simple" Scooby continued. "Women, wives, girlfriends talk. They talk! They like to know what you are doing. Where you are. Whom you are with. Etcetera. Etcetera. And then they want you to ask them how their day was. And about their boring friend Alisha and her Saturday night cooking class. And then about..." Bastard cleared his throat noisily.

"Okay, okay... Point is Hari- you ought to be worried, man" Scooby concluded.

"We are different, Scooby" I replied again, failing to convince myself. Why were all her numbers not working? Why hadn't she called me? Replied to my emails?

Where are you, my fish eyed love?

An MBA campus, in the midst of a recession, is a gloomy place to be. Everybody, everything seems to be frowning. The Profs look more menacing. The reams of abstruse text, you have to go through for some classes, seem all the more pointless and depressing to read.

This was undoubtedly the most depressing period of my life- even more depressing than the days I had spent in my ill fated preparations for IIT-JEE. No one knew where the world was going. No one knew where Meenakshi was.

The conclaves came and went again. The topic of every one of them had something to do with the recession. "Marketing in a recession". "Private Equity & the downturn". "Leveraging IT in a recession". "HR best practices for a meltdown". The speakers wearing expensive suits, boots & watches- appendages quite unbecoming of an economic disaster- spoke of the recession as if it were the White Rabbit in Alice in Wonderland or Barney in HIMYM. As if it were a figment of my now dead pushed-into-a-shoebox imagination; a thing to be talked about, laughed on, enjoyed, savored. I had become the character of the story the speakers- in expensive suits, boots & watches- must tell their families about, over dinner in a fine dining restaurant. *'Did you hear about that chap, Hari? The guy who's MBA got fucked by the recession?'*

The worst part was that people around me seemed as upbeat as the speakers. The recession was a term of economics to them; we were decoupled; FMS was a top ten B-School. No way we're going down, they said. And thus they sat with their hands firmly tucked under their buttocks.

Then one fine day, I got a call on my Nokia.

And my world began to end.

Explode

Beyond the cloud that enveloped my mind, I heard them talking in hushed voices. I heard without listening, words without meaning.

And then a decision was reached. I do not know if it was an agreement, a compromise or Bastard prevailing upon the two of them. Two of them came up to me like kids come up to a mother after breaking expensive crockery. Nobody spoke for a minute and I hoped no one would- that nothing penetrated the cloud that held my mind.

"I'm coming" Bastard said simply.

I didn't know what to say. I hadn't asked any one of them to come with me. But I had hoped that if anyone would, it would be Matar.

"Scooby's got laterals. And Matar's got his chickenpox" Bastard explained.

I nodded.

"You sure you want to miss laterals, Hari?" Matar asked in a weak voice from the bed.

I was not sure of anything anymore. But I nodded.

"Settled then" said Bastard. "Let's leave for the airport."

Kolkata looked at me through thick airplane glasses. As we stepped out, the city was the same- sweaty, hot, filthy, squalid. I was surprised by how much this angered me.

A well built young man in a red T-shirt and a beard met us at Dum Dum Airport. He and Bastard hugged as if they were related or old friends at the very least. I nodded in his direction when Bastard introduced him to me.

Red Shirt packed our sparse luggage in the boot of his van. We followed our luggage into his van; Bastard sat with him in the front and I in the back with a large funny smelling crate that seemed to have been tied in place.

Kolkata came at me through the half open half tainted window of Red Shirt's Omni. The streets were narrower & filthier than I had remembered them to be. We navigated her streets at a deathly slow rate, passed beggars and procrastinators. Off every third building, rose columns of deep dark smoke. I felt thankful for the pollution; it took the edge off Kolkata's stink, her body odor.

Red Shirt kept talking as he drove. I caught random words and sentences off the front. Bastard & Red Shirt appeared to be getting into an argument, but then cooled off and laughed. This happened several times during the journey. Every time their voices would rise to a crescendo and their faces would get contorted by frustration, by disagreement. But then they would cool down inexplicably as if whatever had been said was just a figment of my imagination.

When we reached, it had taken us more time than it had to reach Kolkata by airplane. As we got off, Red Shirt placed his hand on Bastard's shoulder and said "Don't worry. It will be quite… an EXPLOSION."

Red Shirt laughed. And I watched Bastard's face wrinkle into a subtle scowl.

"Do you understand the plan, Hari?" Bastard asked.

I nodded.

"I go in first. I…" Bastard began. "Wait" he said, looking around "Too many people here."

I looked up, across the hall, across the sea of well dressed folk. And then, surrounded by a group of giggling giddy girls, I saw…

"MEENAKSHI!" I shouted.

Everyone, including her, turned and stared at me.

"What the fuck!" Bastard muttered. He took me by the arm and swiftly pushed me into a corner, behind a pillar.

"What the hell Hari!" Bastard exclaimed, still holding me tight by the arm. I stood with him panting, frozen, unsure of what to do next.

We stood by a large somewhat lopsided plaque that screamed "*Rajat Weds Meenakshi*". After a few minutes, my breathing returned to normal. Bastard too had calmed down and said "OK… what we do next is…"

"Hari, what are you doing here?" a musical voice cut Bastard short.

Before I could turn and react, the voice took me by my Bastard free arm and guided me into a small room five paces away. It seemed to be a store room of sorts.

She looked resplendent in her bejeweled sari. I noticed her fish eyes were gone- that she wore lenses. I stared at her- my mind completely blank.

"We don't have much time. I told them I was going to the washroom" she said.

I was struck by how different she looked, sounded. Her voice had a fierce power- a conviction bordering on anger. I was startled by her difference, my brain & rehearsed rage frozen in place.

"Meenakshi" I uttered. "Why?" My brain refused to reproduce the sentences I had rehearsed on the way over. Out of the corner of my eye, I saw Bastard enter the room too.

Meenakshi ogled him awkwardly before asking "Who's this?"

I looked from her to Bastard and then at a bundle of quilt stacked in the corner. Words were not coming to me. I sputtered "Friend" before my brain freeze consumed me again.

"Hari" she said sighing "Why are you here?"

"I... I..." I began before words failed me again.

"We came here to get you" Bastard offered.

"Get me?" she asked innocently. And then realization dawned in her fishless eyes. "Hari... We broke up... remember?" she said softly.

"Broke up?" Shock forced words out of my mouth. I scanned my head for conversations, memories- how mad could I be to have forgotten such a thing?

"You chose, Hari" she said gently. "You chose not to be with me." I saw shadows of tears lurking behind her eyes. She looked away from my gaze.

When? When did I choose? I racked my brains for memories distant & translucent. Was it an email? Was it one of our telephonic conversations? Was it... Was it that day on the park bench?

"That day we met here? That day of the park bench and... and...?" I wondered.

She nodded slightly and whispered "Yes."

The cloud that held my mind blackened, thickened and spewed her with thunder "I ... I didn't want to leave you that day, Meenakshi. I did that... this, MBA, everything- for you. For YOU!"

She sighed softly. "But Hari, I didn't need you to. All I... I needed was you to be with me." She paused as if to fight back tears "My... my father had... I needed you most then, Hari. And you weren't with me." Two tears made their way down her cheeks wreaking havoc on her bridal makeup.

"But... but... I... you" Clouded Brain sputtered.

She wiped her tears on her sari. "Come on, Hari... You are a nice guy. You'll find someone much better than me."

I just looked at her blankly. There was a finality in her voice- I felt I was a lost cause. But I pulled myself together.

"I won't find anyone. I love you alone, Meenakshi" I said simply. "Come with me."

"It's too late, Hari. I can't do this... to Rajat... to my family" she replied. There were more tears in her fishless eyes.

"Goodbye, Hari" she said as she made to leave. "Have a great life." And then she turned to leave.

Bastard held her by the wrist. "Wait! This guy has been in love with you for the last year and a half" he said quietly. "All he talks about is you. Don't do this to him... he will fall to pieces."

"Don't you understand?" she reacted, freeing her arm angrily. "I can't leave like this... especially now. We are not in a movie, Hari."

"Please... please Meena" I pleaded.

"I have to go now" she said without turning to face me. "Or they'll come looking for me." And then she was gone.

I stood motionless rooted in place by shock. Images flashed before my eyes. Kolkata. Battling bulls. A park bench. A mockingbird. Fish Eyes. The voice of music. A wedding not my own. A House of Cards.

The house of cards of my love collapsed and I began to fall as it had. My knees buckled, my legs began to give way. Bastard rushed in to save me from falling.

"What now, Hari?" Bastard asked me.

"Where's the woman?" Red Shirt asked.

Bastard said something. And we got back into the supposed getaway vehicle.

I was struck again by how unsightly Kolkata was- this time the realization was exponentially more pronounced. It came at me again through the van's windows, in all its hideousness, stench and smoke. I now knew that for all the romance it possessed; the city didn't and would never come to anything. It was not Meenakshi, it was me who had been blind- fish eyed all along.

I stayed in my cloud as we made back to the airport, got onto the plane and made for Delhi. I felt a new respect for Delhi; for all its hatred and sliminess, at least the city had been honest with me all along.

We sat on the steps of Delhi Airport waiting for the airline to excrete our luggage. The sun had just begun to set beyond the all glass see-through of the premises. It was of a unique and unusual hue- it was the Sun of Meenakshi's Sorrow.

I stared at the sun, hoping it would give me an answer. Why did this happen to me? How could I have been so blind? What was I to do now?

And then the Sun answered back. It exploded into a million pieces of orange and red.

hear people shrieking, sirens howling, things burning, shattering, all as if they were at a tremendous distance. I saw Bastard's worried face looking at me. I watched his lips move as they said "Hariboy, you OK?" B[illegible]

Half

When I came to, the cloud around my head was gone. It was in the sky spewing rain on the exploded Sun's dying embers.

There was a whole lot of general confusion around me. I could hear people shrieking, sirens howling, things burning, shattering, all as if they were at a tremendous distance. I saw Bastard's worried face looking at me. I watched his lips move as they said "Hariboy, you OK?" But I didn't hear his voice.

And then, I fainted again.

I stood in a huge skyscraper by the glass exterior.

I was far up, quite into the sky. The streets were all empty except for a few figures dressed almost entirely in black.

He was a salesman, selling something out of a shoebox. He wore a black suit piece and his face was in the shadows. Even before I turned, I knew he was behind me and even before he spoke I knew what he was about to say.

"Hari Parmeshwar" he spoke in the words I knew were about to come "Would you like to buy a CDO?" His voice was oddly familiar.

I noticed my lips- who knew it all- silently intoning the words he was speaking. "No thanks" I replied. "Where are we?"

"This is the Watch Tower" he asked and my lips intoned. "You sure about the CDO?"

"You see, my friend" I replied "I know how badly it all ends."

"Everything ends, Hariboy" he rejoindered merrily. And then he flicked a switch on the wall near him and everything around us exploded.

For a second, in the light of everything that burnt, I thought I could see his face. But then he was gone.

"Bastard!"

"Hey Scooby, he's awake!"

It took me a few minutes to open my eyes and I found my voice before I found sight.

"What happened?" I asked.

And again I heard as if the voice were at a tremendous distance. "Terrorist attack" Matar said softly.

My vision was still flickering on. I could make out Scooby sleeping on a chair in the corner. Matar was seated right by my bed; his face was still pockmarked by chickenpox. It appeared to be a room in a hospital.

"At the airport?"

Matar nodded.

"Where's Bastard?" I asked urgently.

"He's in the bed alongside..." Matar said from a distance. I turned my head to find the curtains pulled.

"Is he fine? Did he... did he say something?"

"He got a fucking splinter in the knee but he's fine" Matar replied.

My vision continued to improve gradually. I began to scan my arms, legs for damage. "Matar... how badly hurt am I?"

"Minor cuts & burns mostly" Matar responded. "And your left ear... The Doc said that your hearing will be impaired somewhat, for some time."

I got up or at least tried to get up suddenly. My limbs were quite fast asleep and I almost stumbled to a fall before Matar held me. "Where to, boss?" he asked.

"I need to talk to Bastard... I want to know who... what he... how this happened" I said.

"Well, you'll have to fucking wait till the morning" Matar replied "Coz the nurse gave him some meds and he's fast asleep."

I sat down on the bed again unsure of what to do next. I felt almost certain that it was Bastard I had seen in my dream, making the world explode.

And while I sat down and went over my dream and those words Red Shirt had said, I fainted again.

I woke up in our PG next. I was alone. I had no clue what day it was.

Everything seemed a distant memory. Everything- Meenakshi's rejection, the explosion, the weird Watch Tower of Doom dream, Bastard- seemed inconsequential, far far away, buried somewhere deep. My head had swept it all under a huge carpet and flattened everything out with the rear end of a broom. But there was the blinding realization that something- quite a lot- had gone terribly wrong and that I was changed, perhaps forever.

As I stood up, I noticed that I could see everything with an amazing clarity; every molecule of color there was- every shade, every hue, every minute detail. I was half deaf and half mad but I could see clearer than ever, clearer than perhaps anyone could. And in that period of extraordinary clarity, I understood everything. I knew what had happened. From the corner of my eye, I saw the shoebox that imprisoned my story. I knew what I had to do.

Watch Tower

I half heard voices outside. I walked out and saw that the three of them were on the terrace, gossiping away.

I walked up the stairway quietly. I saw that there was a plate of peanuts & glasses of semi consumed booze between them. Scooby appeared to be busy writing something on a piece of paper.

"Hari!" Matar suddenly exclaimed. "How you feeling?" Bastard & Scooby looked up. I noticed that Bastard's knee was heavily bandaged.

I muttered "Fine" and pushed up a chair to sit with them.

As I sat down, everything paused. They stopped chattering, Scooby stopped writing; I could sense that they had no idea what to say to me- what to do with me. They sat there, doing nothing, avoiding my gaze.

"Guys... What the fuck is up?" I said, smiling slightly.

They all smiled. The ice shattered, the elephant in the room was gone. Matar handed a glass to me.

"Well, we're making a list" Scooby replied.

Bastard cleared his throat. "Scoobster, from the beginning, please..."

Scooby sighed. "Well, while you were gone, we had the worst lats in eight years."

"How many?" I asked, mid beer sips.

"Two" Scooby replied.

"Were you..." I began.

"Nope, not me" Scooby interjected. "Only people placed were an 8.5 and a 9.9. Aastha & Swati."

"Wow" I said.

"You have to accept, guys, that Corporate India doesn't like us" Scooby continued. "Corporate India likes its babes- sexy, bouncy & fresh."

"We've been over this before" Matar retaliated. "I still believe if you're good enough, you get hired."

"Come on, Surdy" Scooby fired back. "That *dopchee* Swati got a 16 lakh job." He paused to take a giant swig of his beer. "And Aastha's idiocy is well known. It all comes down to chest measurements, *bhenchod.* Got boobs? Take job." He banged his bear mug on the table to emphasize his point. A few peanut shells crashed to the floor.

Bastard laughed. "I think it's a vicious slash virtuous cycle, Scoobhead. Being attractive gives your 9's the same amount of confidence that us- less attractive folk- would get from reading hundreds of books. And that, my friends, gives hot babes a tremendous head start on us." He sipped his beer. I had no doubt in my mind form the shade that his beer was that he had- quite needlessly- added some vodka to it. "And yeah, some companies *are* as horny as hell" he concluded, smiling omnisciently.

"Naah... Hot babes have to get in somewhere and when they do, people like you make a fuss about it" Matar said.

"Only two companies came for laterals?" I asked, sidestepping the hot babe issue.

"Four came" Matar replied. "Only two hired."

"Wow" I said softly. "So... what's happening now?"

"What's happening is worldwide destruction, my friend" Scooby replied. "We are all squabbling, fighting, shouting curses at the PlaceCom, screaming *bloody murder*, cursing our fates. But we are doing nothing. There is no damage control. The faculty is fighting amongst itself; the PlaceCom is asking us to wait for finals, which I am sure will be as fucked up as laterals. We are all just waiting for our royal public fucking."

Somewhere in my head a black suited salesman laughed. *Everything ends, Hariboy.*

"And the list?" I inquired.

"Aah, the list..." Bastard said and paused mysteriously.

"The list of Unplaced's" Matar replied.

And then Scooby began to explain. "There are 31 babes... 21 of them relatively hot, at least a 6 on the BM, I mean. With lats and PPO's, 7 outta these 21 are placed. Take that away and you have 14 average to hot-as-hell babes and 16 is the number of people we placed last year in the two days of Slot Zero."

"The point being..." I interjected.

"Point is, my dear HP, put these 14 babes before you and then put the unplaced non-hot-female members of MarkSoc, FinSoc

& ConClub. Then put the freshers" he gestured towards Matar "who, in a normal process, will always get at least twice as many shortlists as us. And then put the toppers, the studs and the not so hot females. Which gives me a figure of 62 people most likely to get placed before me." He took a gloomy swig off his mug of bitter.

"Come on, Scooby, we all know how fucking random placements are" Matar said.

"Speak for yourself, surdy. You are almost a fresher. And this guy" Scooby said, pointing at me "is a fucking Mark God. I am nothing. Nothing!"

"Don't worry, Scooby" I said. "I have no intention to get placed before you."

"Yeah, yeah..." Scooby threw a peanut at me. It missed.

The most important by-product of two years of MBA pain & frolic and the most important input of the bizarre annual game of Placements is a Curriculum Vitae. The average MBA student's CV looks like neatly packed ants crammed into an incredibly small space; as if the kid's done everything in two years- (apparently singlehandedly) organized "National Level" Conclaves, Conferences, etc., advised firms on problems that bamboozled extremely more experienced people, received a Five Star rating in his/ her summer project whilst saving or making millions for his internship company, won big or big sounding events. Almost every CV without fail is an intricate maze of strategically boldened words, exaggerated truths and blatant lies.

No one knows but everyone has an opinion on what the best

format/ design/ look for a CV is. Though PlaceCom sets a prescribed format for CV's, there are still millions of design permutations & combinations possible. Also an eternal & eternally confusing debate on whether to make a one page CV or a two page one, rages constantly before placements.

It is virtually impossible to distinguish between two CV's at a glance because come placements, everybody's CV- for all their differences- begin to look the same; sort of like those pamphlets of Baba Bhola B's Sex & VD Clinic, which come free with your newspaper and which your mind instinctively learns to disregard and gloss over. To add to the confusion, everybody looks the same- in suit, tie, haircut & makeup. And everybody even sounds the same- jargons, abbreviations, frameworks- mostly picked up collectively & hastily in the week before placements. If you can't impress them with your charm, confuse them with your bullshit.

But the CV is the most important edifice of all. It is a singular document for which friendships are forged, enemies made, backs stabbed, bloods donated, randomest possible events participated in (and given positive spins on the aforementioned parchment), societies joined (& for that matter constructed), NGO's founded, hobbies developed (& read about on the net a week before placements), projects done, workshops attended, etcetera etcetera.

For fun, I noted down all my achievements in all my life and was slightly shocked to see that, due to my event winning heroics in second year and a decently accomplished summer project, they ran into two and a half pages. I had a sea of CV points to choose from. I was golden.

Before embarking on sculpting my final CV, I went over Matar & Scooby's CVs. Matar's was a crisp one page document seemingly encapsulating his most important achievements. Scooby's on the other hand was a two page ode to Scoobiness, a CV reeking of awesomeness and bullshit, filled with such laughter inducing points as "CEO's Favorite Employee Award" or "Full Attendance Prize" or "Among Top 13 Marketing Major Laterals" (There were 13 Marketing Major Laterals). His hobbies had to be an amalgamation of Bastard's, Matar's and mine, for I had never known him to follow the stock markets or read Urdu poetry or play percussion & acoustic guitar.

And then I crafted mine. I felt like the Hari Parmeshwar in the Watch Tower looking at my CV a million miles away on the street; and even from that distance, as I saw every word with my new razor sharp vision, it gave me a giddy feeling of happiness- a mad urge to burst out laughing.

I rejoined college a week after the terror attack. I submitted my medicals to avail of attendance exemptions and began to sit in classes, student body meetings & company presentations.

I was still quite half deaf and what the Profs said in class made even less sense than before. The take of the Profs on the recession and the resultant & impending placement slowdown was quite amusing. Several of them believed that by giving us more assignments, forcing us to read/ present on more case studies, they could chase the Recession Monster away. This was predictably of no use at all since academic complications & hirer company requirements rarely ever are the same. Also, by mutual consent and an unspoken code of student community ethics, the work was either shoddily copied from the net or left to the one or more placed people (if any) in the group.

Everybody was an Animal- a meat hungry, rabid, starved hound. And the first target of unbridled fury at FMS- as at campuses across the country- was the PlaceCom. The five young fachhas who we had elected to carry the Great Indian Placement Agency's burden were shouted at, humiliated, berated, argued with and antagonized.

"What is the point of this?" I whispered to Bastard, seated on the side of my good ear.

Bastard sighed but did not respond.

Scooby, seated on my left, hurled a few swearwords I could not quite make out, at those unfortunate PlaceCom scapegoats.

"I agree, HP. There's only so much these kids can do" Bastard said finally.

I nodded in agreement.

"Bastard" I said.

He leant towards me. "What?"

"Tell me about the guy who picked us up at the airport" I said. "How… how do you know him? And why was he talking about an explosion?"

Bastard leaned in and told me his secret.

Mid January, company presentations began in the right earnest. Even without a recession, company presentations are agonizing affairs; but in a recession, they assume singularly painful attributes. As PlaceCom tried to ensure that every last man got placed, the doors of Sem Hall were thrown open to several companies who had never visited us before; and quite possibly never visited an MBA campus before. So we had company executives visiting us in oversized shirts and slippers or talking proudly in painfully broken English about the last year's batch of Management Trainees lifted from "Best B-Schools" like IIPM or Fore School of Management, shooting morale dead at point blank range. One of these angels from industry quite sensed the low morale and "I wish I had died in my sleep today" looks on people's faces and decided to up the mood by shouting "ARE YOU PSYCHED!?" at intermittent intervals. After the initial stream of low volume collective 'Yes'es, Bastard & I began to shout 'NO!' from the back (much to chagrin of the fachha PlaceComie standing guard at the door), putting an end to the stupidity.

But the Legacy Recruiters' (called so because they had been recruiting for as long as anybody could remember) presentations were worse. It was agonizing to sit through them knowing they would at best be taking one lucky bastard from amongst us all. And it was agony on everybody to listen to them sell a product that, come recession, didn't need to be advertised at all.

Case in point was the TAS presentation which is a bi annual B-School event (one before summer and the other before final placements). It is at least 4 hours long; a needless overselling of TAS' merits. I have no doubt in my mind that the presentation is a very important event in the lives of the army of presenters who flies down to present- for they sit and gas around, enjoying every second of eager B-School student 'This is my dream job' spotlight.

I had acquired a laser pointer in my efforts to spice up company presentations. But no amount of highlighting the bald patch on TAS Manager No. 3's head would amuse me that day. So I got up and asked "Excuse me?"

"Yes?" TAS Manager No. 3 said.

"Thank You" I said and made a prolonged & deliberately noisy exit from the Room of Infinite Bright.

As I walked outside, I saw that it was raining in one of Recession's worst storms. And as lightning struck, for a moment I thought I saw him again- the man in the black suit piece trying to sell junk bonds, setting fire to the world. I smiled at him & waved needlessly.

I had now known for some time that that man was me.

Inverse

By now, placement news from other campuses had started to trickle in. Every year, since the dawn of time perhaps, a clutch of consulting companies & I-banks had been picking kids from B-schools across the country, paying atrocious sums of money for the one eyed amongst the blind, allowing B-schools to report unrealistic unearthly average salaries. With these firms now either dead or dying, top dollar recruitments were becoming an exception rather than the norm. To aggravate the situation further, the talent that would have gotten absorbed by these now lifeless bigwigs, was now crowding into the recruitment processes of those more earthly firms, filling a space henceforth held only by mediocre or damned kids. Placement processes were crashing like dominoes.

Closer home, with placements lurking around the corner & the PlaceCom forecasting doom, everybody got down to ruthless mugging. Scooby who had taken both finance & marketing subjects in his desire to take a dual degree (and hence have a shot at every company that came to campus), now had a mountain of books, journals, blogs, concepts, formulae, etc. to go through. Matar, who like me had taken only marketing subjects throughout the second year, had a somewhat less onerous task before him of mugging up Kotler, reading up on brands, memorizing marketing frameworks & big sounding words- anything that could be thrown around & sound good in a Group Discussion.

It was in one of these mugging symposiums at our PG that Bastard chanced upon my CV.

"Whoa!" Bastard exclaimed. "That's your CV, HP?"

I laughed. "Hell yeah it is." Scooby snatched the sheet from Bastard's hand.

"This is… um…" Bastard snapped his fingers as if he were missing the right word.

"Wow" Scooby said softly. Matar was now onto it too.

"Fucking bullshit!" he exclaimed.

Loud snap. "The *sexiest* CV I have ever seen" Bastard finished.

Matar shook his head violently. "No no no no no! What the fuck is this, Hari?"

"My CV" I replied.

Scooby pointed to the lower half of my CV and began laughing.

"Why is *everything* in fucking bold?" Matar continued, his cheeks reddening with indignation.

"Not to mention, all your achievements are from…" Scooby interjected, still giggling. "Class 5th or before. Whoa! You won a TT match in 1st standard! How?"

"This makes no fucking sense at all" Matar said.

"Yeah. You wouldn't even have reached the top of a TT table in 1st standard" Scooby added.

"Not that, Scoob" Matar said. "I mean what's with the bullshit CV?"

I smiled without replying.

"And… and what's with you walking out of company ppts? And not really preparing for placements? What the fuck is on, HP?" Matar's face combined worry & fury. "Who are you, Hari? I mean who *are* you now?"

"Matar, my fucking friend" I said "I *am* the recession's oppositely charged mate."

"Fucking fuck fuck…" He took a few deep breaths to calm himself. "Okay, your girlfriend left you. You were… you were in a terror blast thing. But that doesn't mean you do… you go mad!"

"Don't worry, Matar" I replied calmly. "I am not mad."

"Oh yes you are mad, HP" Scooby spoke pointing to my CV "Fancy dress winner. Poetry recitation champion." Bastard chuckled.

"All I know is" Matar went on "You are not the Hari Parmeshwar who left on that plane."

"Of course I am not" I retorted smiling. "My girlfriend left me. I was in a terror blast thing."

Matar sighed. "Come off it, HP, please" he pleaded. His cheeks were cherry red now, under his beard.

"Did TAS reveal its salary?" I asked.

"Hunh? What does that have to fucking do with anything?" Matar replied.

"I know it didn't, Matar. Scooby told me" I continued. "And doesn't that make you angry at some level? Four hours of gas and they don't even tell you the salary?"

"Of course it makes me fucking angry Hari!" he retorted irately. "But less angry than I am at you right now."

I laughed, irritating him & his cheeks further. "Matar, I am not insane. I am just… *angry*. Very angry."

"You don't look angry to me HP" Scooby countered.

I shrugged. "I can see now, Matar" I said. "And I can only hear half everything."

"So?"

"So I have stopped listening to the world" I answered. "And I see everything clearer than ever."

"Again, so?" he asked, cheeks redder than ever.

I smiled omnisciently. "Matar, I am more sure than I have ever been that this is what I have to… what I am meant to do."

"Bullshit!" Matar exclaimed.

"And what is it that you are meant to do, HPMan?" Bastard asked.

I reminisced over the answer I had prepared in my head a while ago and I spoke something completely different in its stead. "I am just a man in a black suit."

"Hunh?" Matar said.

"As I see it Matar" I continued this time with my prepared answer "given that placements have no fucking meaning for me anymore… don't look shocked Matar, they really don't. So given that, I have two choices before me. One, I sign out of the process which is the dull, dreary, no- fun way of going about it. Or Two" I went on, holding up two of my fingers "I sit through the process with no intention of getting placed and get some fun out of it."

"And of course, you choose the latter" Bastard summed up.

The man in the black suit smiled & nodded.

The evening of that day, our batch went face to face with the PlaceCom in what is an annual sham called the "Expectation Setting GBM". There was a furore as PlaceCom gave out the names of expected companies on campus. With placements less than a week away, even if all the companies listed came to campus (which was virtually impossible; every year only about 50% of "Confirmed" companies turn up), we would still be short by at least ten people.

PlaceCom told us all about how bad it was going to be. They told us an expected salary figure that was lower than the average salary several freshers had left at their engineering campuses, lower than my last salary at ABC. They told us how companies didn't want to hire anymore; and if they did, all they wanted to hire was the one best kid from IIMA. They told us how even several of our seniors were either being fired or kept on extended probation.

Everybody shouted. They shouted at the PlaceCom for being inefficient, for not being creative enough, for attending too many classes (& hence not devoting enough time to placement work). For FMS not being IIMA. For there being a recession.

The five juniors listened to the ranting and raving with some patience. They stayed calm. At first. Then they went into a huddle and came back at us. They ranted and raved themselves. They blamed us for not being prepared enough. For being unkempt or sleeping through company presentations. For asking stupid questions. For souring relations with companies. They offered to resign.

It was the last straw for both sides of the fence. The intensity of ranting & raving reduced, people quietened down a bit. And then, when most anger had been spewed, they all went home resigned to their damned fates.

There is a famous and oft abused saying at FMS about placements- "The process will take care of itself". Rest assured, it does not.

"Taking care" of the placement process is the entity already introduced as the PlaceCom. How the cycle of placements works every year is that the senior team places the junior batch in their summer internships. A junior team is then elected in place, which has the onerous task of placing the senior batch before it.

In a B-School, a PlaceCom member is all powerful- he/ she has the power to push/ pull your CV into/ out of placement processes of companies and to sweet talk companies into hiring you or conversely, to turn them against you- all in an endeavor to ensure cent percent placements. Besides this, a member of the PlaceCom will have access to truckloads of critical information- for example, what kind of CV's work with which kind of companies, what kind of people a certain company is looking for, what are some of the things a certain company would like to hear from a candidate, etc.

Since the dawn of time, PlaceCom members have found ways to abuse their positions. Getting friends critical info/ shortlists/ jobs, keeping enemies out. It is easy to do and impossible to trace. Only about one in a hundred such transgressions (or less) get caught out and even if they do or did in the past, they are or had been blind-eyed because placements turned out to be awesome anyway.

So, to digress from my present digression, in the second week of February began the placement process that would not and could not take care of itself. We all showed up in suits, boots, ties and haircuts to campus. Over time, I have developed and fine tuned a theory on suits, which I might have mentioned previously. Suits make you look good. People who look good in normal clothes, look even better. MBAkinds (probably) wear suits because it is difficult to say 'No' to a beggar in a suit. Sure he knows nothing, but at least his tie is top notch.

And we sat in those little swivel chairs made without comfort in mind, all suited- booted for those hirers that were brave enough to hire in the recession. We sat and waited for companies to show up. This was Day Zero, reserved exclusively for the best or (actually) the most hyped firms. TAS, HUL, Citi, Standard Chartered, P&G (dead i-Banks excluded) - to name a few.

Several of these Day Zee firms had already released the shortlists for their processes. Now, no one has any clue whatsoever how companies shortlist candidates year after year. You can be a class topper with an incredibly weighty CV and not be shortlisted. Conversely, you can be a gaseous guy who knows absolutely nothing, your biggest achievement being making it to FMS and still get a shortlist. I have no doubt in my mind that someone in the Human Resources Department of these firms sits year after year and since every bloody CV looks about the same, makes up some kind of random rule (for example, *this year we won't hire anyone whose name starts with S, M, B or P*) to justify his atrocious salary and to eliminate a majority of those that applied.

Hence it so happens that I (having a name beginning with 'H') got two shortlists on Day Zero despite having an atrocity of a CV while Matar got just one & Scooby got none at all. In contrast, every unplaced member of the senior PlaceCom had shortlists from *every* Day Zero company. Ruchi, who was the class topper now, too got just one and could be heard bitching about the sinister inside bunglings of the PlaceCom (in getting their senior chums shortlists).

My first Group Discussion was TAS which is an hour long severe pain inducing process involving ten case discussions in quick succession. Now there is more to my getting a shortlist from TAS than the mysterious ways of the Shortlist World or the inside workings of the PlaceCom. I had deliberately filled the TAS form seriously- writing up all sorts of gas about mission, vision, social contribution, long term/ short term bullcrap. I wanted to see the carnage firsthand, I wanted to be a part of the madness.

I firmly believe that nothing constructive can ever come out of a monitored Group Discussion in India. I needn't have worried about maddening the GD because everybody was quite mad, jumped up, desperate, willing to slit throats for their dream job. They looked at each other suspiciously, disregarded each other's points, "begged to differ", jumped to the solution without getting to the problem. It was the Coloseum and the emperors from TAS looked at my Gladiators gaily, as they let out each other's blood and guts.

I got in a few times making random statements about interlinkages, monetary policy, socio economic equilibrium- basically any word that sounded too big to be wrong. At one point, I pretended to have taken personal offense at a statement from somebody, causing him to apologize profusely to me. I had already said "No!" abruptly when one of the Gladiators rather belligerently asked me to elaborate on the connection that monetary policy had with the case at hand. By the time we were onto the seventh case, I was too bored to have fun anymore. I just sat there doing & saying nothing, shining the sun in everybody's eyes with my watch. When the sham ended, the Gladiators shuffled back to our room, bruised and battle weary.

My next GD was HUL which is the dream job of any marketing MBA worth his salt. Half the senior MarkSoc team was in my GD. The panel, comprising of one young hotshot Levers guy of two years, gave us a case to read, with a few questions at the end. And then I saw them at their worst. Yet.

Four people jumped to start the GD. And for a whole minute, none of them shut up. It sounded like a whole other language. I heard random words- SWOT, Segmentation, Positioning, Sales, superfluous, etc. without any of it making any sense at all. The panelist shut the process down, asked everybody to calm down and take another two minutes.

When the GD restarted, it got worse. This time, five people started simultaneously. I added to the confusion shouting random words- 'interlinkages', 'monetary policy', 'socio economic equilibrium', my throwaround words of the day, at intermittent intervals. I could only half hear everything but I am sure that the GD must have sounded like a confused many-headed beast with a digestive system that did not quite agree with him.

Within five minutes, HUL hotshot had had enough. He asked everybody to shut up & leave.

I got no interview calls. Neither did Matar. Day Zero ended with nine people placed. I went home and watched 'Gladiator' on my laptop.

From thereon, the rest of the process I remember as a block, rather than as segregated into Days. Primarily because from Day Zero on, it heated up to another level of Mad.

In the entire process, only four FMCG's (the dream recruiters for Marketing MBA's) showed up against a historic average of at least fifteen. To add to the melodrama, Marketing companies offered Finance profiles and Finance companies (banks) vice versa. Everything went from 'Dream Job' to "My Dream is to have a Job' for the Gladiators.

My shortlists dwindled now with the impact of my joker CV being felt. But I still managed to land a shortlist here and there and have my fun befuddling the Gladiators & the panel. As people were beginning to see a pattern to my randomness, I had to evolve my strategy to make my ramblings more subtle. This meant that despite my quite obvious madness, I landed up with one or two interview calls.

From what I learnt & what I now know, among the initial few questions every company without fail will ask you is why you want to join them. It is impossible to have an answer ready for each & every one of the recruiters; so it pays to have one or two generic answers that can be applied everywhere. Use the words, "Challenging/ entrepreneurial environment", "steep learning curve", "atmosphere that encourages creativity/ innovation/ initiative", "largest company/ sector", "fastest growing company/ sector", etcetera etcetera and usually you would be home free.

I had my fun with the interviews. I told a marketing company I wanted to work finance and retire within two years. I started negotiating my prospective salary with them- telling them 7 lakhs was simply not tenable. I told them I was a Marketing God, that I knew everything and then stayed silent through or said "I have no clue" if they asked me marketing questions.

My final shortlist/ interview of the placement process was with a weird unheard of company offering a weird unheard of profile. As I entered and sat down, a good looking HR woman asked me to describe myself. Now I had prepared a really funny "Describe yourself" answer but my brain faltered & tracking back to recent memory, I offered something else in its stead.

"I am Maximus Decimus Meridius" I began.

When the process officially ended, about thirty people remained unplaced- Matar, Scooby & me among them. The process had now become what is known as "Rolling" which means companies come as and when they please, instead of in a time band of a few days.

The junior PlaceCom was disbanded and the Placement Secretary, Sandeep (one of our batch) took over. With a month to go to end of session, on the request of the Placement Secretary, us- downtrodden unplaced folk- went to see the Dean to appeal for his help.

Room Of Sepulchral Shadows

The Dean sat in his chair running his fingers through his French beard. He wore thick glasses set in an old fashioned Communist style cheap frame. His eyes looked at us with some contempt as twenty five of us- mostly lateral candidates- filled into his chambers.

His room was quite ill lit. It was dark, depressing, dungeon like- a tomb more than a room- gloomy, moody and somewhat ill. It was a room of Sepulchral Shadows.

Scooby began by stating the obvious "Sir, we have not been placed."

The Dean tapped his fingers on the desk and continued to look at us intently without responding.

Some of us stared back at him. Others looked around at his room & its gloomy ill lit majesticity.

"Sir, ac… actually" Mithun began this time "we… we came here… came to…"

"I know why you are here" the Dean said, baring his tobacco yellowed teeth. He then got back to stroking his Frenchie and staring at us wordlessly.

I felt bored. I had no place here; nothing to beg him for- no request to make. My only motivation in being here was a teensy bit of curiosity and the fact that Matar & Scooby were as yet unplaced.

Suddenly he got up and began to pace the room in the little space that was left, his hands behind his back. "This is not a placement agency" he said in a quiet yet disturbing tone, baring his yellow fangs.

"I can do nothing for you. Contact the Placement Convener" he said.

I stared at him in shock, unsure if he was really saying the words he was saying or if my half mad head was making it all up. But I saw that look of shock reflected on everyone's faces and I knew it was all quite real.

"We are an academic campus. Our focus is management theory" he continued in his voice that somehow combined quietude & disquiet. "My job is to educate you, not to get you jobs."

"But… but s… s… sir" Mithun began.

The Dean raised a hand to silence him. "If you wanted a job, you should have never left one to come here. I am sorry. There is nothing I can do to help" he said, with conclusiveness in his voice. "You can all leave now." He sat down in his throne and began to go at his computer with his mouse.

People started to shuffle out. "All you have to do is give them your contacts" I said suddenly.

He looked up from the screen. People stopped in their tracks. "What?" Yellow Fangs asked.

"Give PlaceCom your corporate contacts. Or send that mail to the rest of the faculty requesting them to share their's" I went on.

"As I have already told you, placements is not my responsibility" he replied, heating up. "Contact the Convener!"

Matar started tugging at my arm but I wasn't finished. "You are the *Dean*- the CEO. Everything is your responsibility!"

"What is your name, *sir*?" he asked.

"Hari" I replied instantly.

"I remember you" he said. "Hari Parmeshwar, isn't it?" He had been in my FMS interview panel.

I nodded.

"Well, Mr. Parmeshwar, if you have any issue with me you are free to take it up with the University Vice Chancellor" he said calmly. "But leave now."

"No" I said.

"No?" Yellow Fangs asked.

"As I see it, *sir*" I continued "you are honor bound to place us."

"Hunh?"

"If placements are not the *focus* here, why did the brochure not say so?" I asked. "Why did it highlight the fact that FMS has always had 100% placements and that the average salary had jumped 15%? As I see it, I paid for that brochure and that brochure is our contract. You are contractually bound to place us."

He tapped his fingers irritably on his desk. "Mr. Parmeshwar!

You guys do not attend lectures! You do not read! And then you expect to get placed? Leave now or I will suspend you from campus!"

I stood resolute staring at him hard. Everybody else stayed rooted too, watching in partial shock as this unusual altercation unfolded.

"Nothing to lose" I muttered.

"WHAT!" he shouted.

"You see, sir, I have lost everything in my two years here at FMS" I replied. "I have nothing left to lose. You can suspend me but I would still be standing here arguing with you." I sighed. "All you have to do is send *one goddamn email.*"

"Mr. Parmeshwar!" he yelled furiously. "I will not have you dictate what I have to do! I am suspending you from classes for one month. And if you" he pointed to those around me "do not empty my office within the next thirty seconds, I will suspend you all too! LEAVE!"

They started to shuffle out. And as they all left, I was the only one left behind- a lone man wearing a black suit in the recesses of my mind. I walked up to Yellow Fangs and whispered "Everything ends" and smiled.

As I stepped out of the Room of Sepulchral Shadows, I felt more alive and awake than I had ever had in my life. Freeing myself from the milling crowd of unplaced souls, I descended down the entrance stairs into a pall of dust & smoke and Delhi's mad roads.

Outside a man in an expensive sedan had grazed a motorcycle. They stood in the middle of the road- fighting, threatening to kill each other, abusing each other's female relatives. Traffic was backed up for half a kilometer. It was utter chaos.

I felt completely at home.

I went to my PG and found the shoebox I was looking for. I had a story to finish.

Epilogue

Two months after session ended, I got published. '*Son of God*' went on to be a national bestseller. More importantly however, my publisher handed me a three book contract- which meant they were going to publish me thrice, no matter what- recession or no recession.

Matar & Scooby both got placed eventually. They actually landed up pretty decent jobs considering it was a rolling process. Last heard, Matar was looking to change jobs.

I am going to this auditorium in Delhi today. Matar and Scooby are coming too. There is going to be a performance by "The Explosion"- a punk rock band. Bastard is the drummer, Rashid (Red Shirt) the vocalist. Bastard said they were going to devote a song to me- for going half mad, for renouncing the unhappy mirage that would have been a job and following my dream. For keeping "The Explosion" a secret. Till today.

As I sit back in my cab, completely at peace with the world, hearing fully now but half mad forever, I hear a song come over the radio.

"At least we're dreaming,
At least we're alive.
As long as we're free men
everything's gonna be alright."